under
the
mesquite

under
the
mesquite

Guadalupe Garcia McCall

LEE & LOW BOOKS INC. • NEW YORK

Tree image on front cover and leaf motif on interior pages and back cover
adapted from photographs by Guadalupe Garcia McCall.

Earlier versions of four poems previously appeared in the following publications:

The Concho River Review (Vol. XII, No. 1, Spring 1998): "En Los Estados Unidos" and "Mi Madre";
Entre Nous (June 1998): "Elotes";
Bueno (In One Ear Publications) (Vol. VII, No. 4, Summer 1998): "En Los Estados Unidos";
The Dirty Goat (Vol. 10, 1999): "Swimming the Rio Grande."

Thanks to the hardworking editors at these literary magazines for finding
un rinconcito within the pages of their journals for my poetry—G.G.M.

Definition of *mesquite* on page v adapted from:

Feller, Walter. "Mesquite," Mojave Desert Plants: Trees. http://mojavedesert.net/trees/mesquite

Ramos, Mary G. "The Ubiquitous Mesquite." Texas Almanac (2006–2007).
http://www.texasalmanac.com/health/mesquite-tree.html

The Random House College Dictionary, Revised Edition. New York: Random House, Inc., 1988.

Manufactured in the United States of America by Worzalla Publishing Company, February 2012

Book design by Kimi Weart
Additional design work by Christy Hale
Book production by The Kids at Our House

The text is set in Perpetua
10   9   8   7   6   5   4   3   2
First Edition

Library of Congress Cataloging-in-Publication Data
McCall, Guadalupe Garcia.
Under the mesquite / by Guadalupe Garcia McCall. — 1st ed.
p. cm.
Summary: Throughout her high school years, as her mother battles cancer,
Lupita takes on more responsibility for her house and seven younger siblings, while
finding refuge in acting and writing poetry. Includes glossary of Spanish terms.
ISBN 978-1-60060-429-4 (hardcover : alk. paper)
[1. Coming of age—Fiction. 2. Responsibility—Fiction. 3. Family life—Texas—Fiction.
4. Cancer—Fiction. 5. Mexican Americans—Texas—Fiction. 6. Texas—Fiction.] I. Title.
PZ7.M47833752Und 2011
[Fic]—dc22   2010052567

I

mesquite (meh-SKEET *or* MES-keet)
[from Spanish *mezquite*, originally from Nahuatl *mizquitl*]

A sturdy tree or shrub with sweet, beanlike pods, sharp thorns, and extraordinarily long roots, native to the southwestern United States and northern Mexico. To survive in harsh climates, the mesquite can adapt to almost any soil, can endure droughts by reaching deeper than other trees to find water, and can grow back from even a small piece of root left in the ground.

Este libro está dedicado con mucho cariño
a la memoria de mi madre, Tomasa Ruiz de Garcia—
porque siempre estarás en mi corazón.

In loving memory of my mother,
Tomasa Ruiz de Garcia—
because you will always be in my heart.

And to my sons,
James, Steven, and Jason—

You've brought immense joy and love into
my life. May these poems bring you closer
to understanding the strength you have
within you; and may you find the courage to
live, laugh, and love with all your heart, here
en los Estados Unidos, or wherever else life
may take you.

Love,
MOM

contents

under
the
mesquite

PART ONE

the weight of words

the story of us

Eagle Pass, Texas
Freshman year of high school

I am standing just inside
the doorway, watching Mami talk
to the television screen.
As the latest episode
of her favorite *telenovela* unfolds,
the soap opera drawing her in,
the skins from the potatoes
she is peeling
drop into her apron
like old maple leaves.

I wait until
she is too busy to notice—

eyes, lips, and heart

all fixed on the television.

Seizing the moment, I tiptoe

into Mami's bedroom

and sneak into her closet.

Eyes shimmering, I am

a ratoncita, a sly little mouse.

I reach into her old purse,

the one that has sat

in her closet for years.

I know no money hides there—

she keeps that

in her newer purse,

the one she takes everywhere.

No, today I am Eve in the garden,

stealing *secretos*,

mining for knowledge,

hoping for a taste

of the forbidden fruit.

A click of the purse's clasp

and my hand, novice thief,

draws out official documents.

A dried-out rubberband
snaps—no warning,
just a bite that smarts.
Folded wings of paper
tremble in my hands
like frightened doves.
My ravenous eyes
greedily devour the words
inscribed on birth certificates,
a marriage license,
a Mexican passport.

But nothing about the *secreto*
I know she is keeping from us.
No new discoveries,
no revelations,
just a crumpled tissue
inside a plastic bag
that sighs quietly
as I lift it out of Mami's purse.
The tissue blossoms in my palm
to reveal a tangled brown mass,
wrinkled, leathery, and dry,

the length of it held together
with a yellowed plastic
medical clamp.
Startled and repulsed,
I drop it.

I am on my knees,
trying to pick it up with the tissue
without actually having to touch it,
when Mami walks in
and catches me in the act.
My face burns with shame,
and fear grips my limbs.
I can't move.

But instead of getting mad,
Mami laughs.
She helps me stand up
and says, "This is probably
going to sound strange. . . ."
Then she takes the shriveled thing
in her hands and tells me

it is her *tesoro*.

"It's your umbilical cord,
Lupita, a treasure I keep
to remind me of the tie
that binds us together.
You were my first baby,
my first love."

Hearing her explain it that way,
I'm not grossed out
by the cord anymore.
"What about Papi?" I ask teasingly.
"I thought *he* was your first love."

For a second I catch a glimpse
of that same secret smile
I've seen on Mami's face
when Papi comes up behind her
while she's at the kitchen sink
and he starts to sing to her
a soft love song
like Pedro Infante.

"Well," Mami says, looking
at me now, "that's different."

She wraps the cord carefully
in the tissue, puts it in its plastic bag,
and hands it back to me.

"This," she says, "is the story of us."

thorns

I was born at home,
in our little blue house
on Avenida López Mateos,
in Piedras Negras, Coahuila, Mexico.
Even though there was no doctor there
because I came so quickly
and unexpectedly,
I arrived perfectly healthy.
Mami says I was so strong,
I didn't act like a newborn.

By the time my sister Analiza
was born the year after,
I was already walking and talking.
Victoria came along two years later,

and then my brother Paco the next year.
When I was six years old,
our family left our beloved Mexico
and moved to *los Estados Unidos*.

In our backyard in Texas,
Papi planted a tall mulberry tree
to shade us in the afternoons.
Mami planted a garden
in our front yard: rosebushes,
rows and rows of them,
all the way down to the street.

It's been more than eight years
since my parents transplanted us,
and our family has grown.
The four youngest kids—
my sisters Tita, Juanita, and Rosita
and my baby brother, Benito—
were born here.
We've been pretty happy,
living the American Dream
in Eagle Pass,

this bilingual border town
most of us call El Águila.

But lately Mami's changed.
A thorny mesquite has sprouted
in the middle of her rose garden.
Even after she has pulled it out
by its roots repeatedly,
pricking herself on its thorns each time,
it keeps growing back.
Today the resilient mesquite
causes her to cry with frustration.
I abandon the journal
I've been writing in
to kneel beside her on the grass
and put my arms around her.

After a few minutes Papi comes over
and tells Mami gently,
"Leave it alone, *mi amor*.
It's in the tree's nature
to be stubborn. It's a survivor.
Come on, it's getting late.

Let's go inside." He coaxes her
away from the rose garden.

Papi says the mesquite is nice to have.
He says someday
when the eight of us kids are all grown
and the tree is sturdy and tall,
Mami will come to appreciate
its simple beauty
among her delicate roses.

With Papi about to go work
on a new carpentry job
far away from home again
and Mami looking more troubled every day,
I think that fiesty little mesquite
is the least of our problems.

something's different

Despite the beautiful unfurling
of new spring buds and leaves,
Mami seems distracted.
Worry lines burden her forehead
day and night no matter how hard
I try to make her smile.
Her heavy sighs
brush against our skin
when we walk by,
and she reaches for us
for no reason at all,
holding us in a fierce embrace.

While Mami sits at the kitchen table
with her two closest *comadres*,

Lucía and Serafina,
we sit on the floor with their kids
playing *lotería*,
our *tablas* set up like bingo cards.
By the doorway, we are
just far enough away not to hear
what they are whispering about.
Still, I can't help but notice
the anxious, sympathetic glances
Mami's friends are giving her.

The room I share with Victoria
is the one closest to
Mami and Papi's bedroom.
Victoria usually climbs into her bed
and falls asleep as soon as the lights
are off. But not me.
Most nights I lie awake,
listening to the soft breathing
of Victoria sleeping
peacefully beside me.
Tonight, however, I hear
Mami in the other room,

trying to smother
the sound of her crying
by having the television on low,
and the murmur of Papi's voice
comforting her
the way I wish I could.

chismosa

I thought I was being clever
by sitting just outside the kitchen window,
but I was wrong.

"¡Chismosa!" Mami chastises me
when she catches me eavesdropping
on her and her *comadres*.
Then she orders me to go scrub
the bathrooms, toilets and all.

After her friends leave,
Mami calls me into her and Papi's room.
"You embarrassed me today,"
she says, sitting on the edge of the bed
with her arms folded.

I sit down cautiously beside her.
"*Secretos* should not be kept
from the oldest daughter," I tell her.

"You may be the eldest, Lupita,
but there are some things
you are too young to understand,"
she says firmly, her face still angry—
disappointed.

"I know I shouldn't have
been listening," I admit.
"But I've been worried about you.
Mami, I'm good for more than
changing diapers and putting little ones
to sleep. I can bear up when things
go wrong. You're the one
who raised me to be that way."

Mami puts her arms around me.
Then she kisses my temple
and rocks me back and forth
as if I were a baby.

But I haven't been her baby
in fourteen years.

"It's okay," I whisper
against her cheek. "I know."
My heart aches
because I have heard the word
that she keeps tucked away
behind closed doors.

"What do you know?" Mami asks.

We lock eyes,
and she knows I know.

"Don't tell the others," she begs,
and I hold her while she cries it out.

the talk

"You know what this means,
   don't you?" Mireya says
   on our way home from school.

My best friend is staring at me
   like I just slapped the pope.

"What?" I ask, looking away,
   pretending this is just a routine
   conversation between *amiguitas*.

"She's going to die."

"No, she's not!" I insist,
   stopping midstride to glare at her.

"Yes, people with cancer die, Lupita."

"She's having an operation,"
  I inform Mireya,
  walking on ahead of her.

"When?" Mireya presses,
  catching up to me as I round a corner.

"Soon." The word leaves my mouth
  quietly, tentatively, because I'm afraid
  to talk about it.

"That doesn't mean she's
  going to beat it," Mireya says.
"People with cancer usually die."

  As we stand at an intersection,
  her words rattle around in my head
  like an old dime
  tumbling down an empty well,
  and I feel hollow inside.
  I press the heel of my shoe

against the dirt
and listen to the crunch
of thin twigs and leaves breaking
under the weight of my foot.
The silence between us
is unbearable.

"We can't be friends anymore," I tell her,
blinking away my tears.

"I'm not trying to be mean, Lupita.
I'm trying to prepare you," Mireya says.

She's as ruthless as a rattlesnake,
but she can't just open her big, fat mouth
and expect me to let her poison me.

"Mami's never liked you," I snap.
"Now I know why."

the sacrifice

It's Wednesday, and like every
Wednesday after school, I am
preparing for my confirmation.
First we go to class
at the Sacred Heart Church annex
and listen to Mother Magdalena's lecture.
Then we practice our prayers
and give thanks in the chapel.

I walk past the chapel's ten
stained glass windows
shining brilliantly
in the afternoon sun,
toward the colossal carved figure
of the resurrected Jesus
suspended high above the altar.

I take a seat in the front row
because it's too crowded
in the back, and right now
I need to be alone.

Kneeling in the pew,
my fingers knotted together like rope,
I beg Jesucristo for a miracle.
In two weeks
Mami is going to have
an operation to remove
the cancer growing in her uterus.
Today I barter with God.
"I'll do anything
if you let Mami live," I promise
as tears roll down my face.

Up to this point in my life
faith has always strengthened me,
stilled my fears, soothed my pain.
Now I am filled with doubts—
and hungry for a sign of mercy,
knowing that only God
can keep Mami from dying.

"Anything," I whisper.
"I'll dedicate my life to you.
Just . . . please . . . don't let her die."

When I finally stop praying
long enough to take a breath
and lift my head,
Victoria comes over, sits down
next to me, and rubs my back.
Even though she's still in middle school,
we're in the same catechism class.
I missed two years of instruction
because I was helping Mami at home.
Victoria covers the side of her face
with her hand so that the others
won't notice we're both crying.
But it's no secret;
thanks to Mireya, everyone knows
our mother has cancer.

When we return to the annex
for the second half
of this week's lecture,
a nun we've never seen before

enters the room. We all sit back.
She says she is here to tell us
about her vocation,
then asks if there are any
among us who would like to do
God's work by devoting
their lives to the faith.
Joyously, I wipe away my tears,
smile, and raise my hand.

Later in the afternoon
two young nuns
come to our home.
Mami welcomes them.
They sip *limonada* with us
in the living room.
But when they ask her
for permission to take me away,
put me in a convent,
and teach me to become a nun,
tears glisten against Mami's cheeks
like clear rosary beads.
She shakes her head.
"No," Mami says emphatically.

"We've made other plans.
Lupita's a gifted writer. She's going
to community college."

And with that the nuns are gone.

I go to my room,
throw myself down on my bed,
bury my face in the pillow,
and cry miserably.

Mami comes in and tries to talk to me.
"Don't be disappointed," she begs.

"Stop trying to run my life!"
I scream, pulling away
because I can't tell her
how scared I am of losing her.

"Trust me," she says, stroking my hair,
pushing it away from my hot face.
"Someday you'll thank me for this."

PART TWO

remembering

six years old

Piedras Negras, Coahuila, Mexico

I remember Mami
sitting in a rocking chair
with her black hair plaited
into a long, silky braid
and her eyes, the golden brown of honey,
watching the horizon
as she rocked herself happily on the porch
of our tiny blue house in Mexico.
Across a busy street,
behind the *plaza de toros*,
where we went to watch
the bullfights sometimes,
a *nopalera*, a colony of crabby cacti,
had been calling to her all morning.
Mami, pregnant with her fifth *bebé*,

was *antojada*, a victim of her food cravings.
She wanted nothing more
than a meal of *nopales en salsa*,
the soft flesh of tender cactus pads
peeled and diced, then sautéed
in a spicy tomato sauce.

So she sat the four us on the bed
and slid our feet into our shoes.
Since I was the oldest, it was my job
to hold Analiza's and Victoria's hands
as we left the house.
With Paco cleaved high on her hip,
Mami led the way.
We stood at the edge of the road
as vehicles roared by
and drove that hot, summer wind
right into our faces.
It felt as if we waited a lifetime
before we could finally cross—
four baby chicks clinging to
the Little Red Hen
by the hem of her skirt,
with her clucking the whole time.

Once we were safely across the street,
we followed a dirt path
until we stood at the top of a hill,
looking down into a wide valley.
Below us, at the end of the world
it seemed, we finally saw them—
hundreds of cacti huddled together.
The only thing that separated
our family from theirs
was an old barbed wire fence.
Mami handed Paco to me.
Facing the parallel lines of wire,
she pushed the bottom wire down
with a sandaled foot.
Then carefully, with her hands,
she pulled the other wires up
until they were bent far enough apart
for us to slip between them.
We climbed through quickly, eagerly,
like ants to a feast.

the gift of words

When we lived in Mexico,
Papi was never home. He worked
all week across the border,
en los Estados Unidos.
On Friday nights I'd watch
from the window, waiting impatiently
for him to come home.

It was Papi who first told me
I had the gift of words.
One night he said it was time
to put them on paper.
He opened Mami's old blue suitcase,
pulled out his notebook,
and leafed through

his sketches of horses,
which he worked on at night.
I caressed them as they galloped by,
page after beautiful page,
until he came to the blank pages at the back.

Papi's hand guided mine
as I clutched the pencil,
holding it sideways against my fingertips.
"The S is a *serpiente*, sitting up
on its tail," he told me.
Then we made the letter C,
curled up like a tiny bug, a *cochinilla*.

"You have a talent for letters,"
Papi said, speaking softly in my ear.
His hands were rough and scratchy
against my skin, and the bits of sawdust
clinging to his work clothes
were tiny mosquitoes biting into my arms.
But his voice was sweet and gentle.
My pencil whispered the letters
onto the paper like magic.

Words, Papi said, would make me
successful when we went to live
en los Estados Unidos
and I went to school there.
He and I practiced our English—
"Hello,"
        "Good-bye,"
                "Thank you"—
words that tasted like lemon drops,
tart and sweet at the same time.

"I don't want to go," I cried,
hugging Papi and hiding my face
in his sunburned neck. "It's too far,
and there won't be any sunflowers
to play with in the yard."

"We'll plant flowers together.
You'll love it then," Papi promised,
and he put away the notebook
in the suitcase, where Mami also kept
our brand-new green cards: our tickets
into *los Estados Unidos*.

uprooted

When I peeked out the windows
in our new house
across the Rio Grande,
the lawns looked well behaved
and boring. The grass grew obediently
beside the clean sidewalks
along the paved streets,
each green blade standing upright
like a tiny soldier.

At first what I missed most
were *los girasoles*,
my tall, unruly friends
with their bright yellow petals
and dark brown faces

always looking up
at the wide blue sky.
When Mami came looking for me
in the afternoons,
I used to suppress my giggles
as I hid behind
those wild sunflowers.

It made me sad to know
that from our new home
I could not hear their voices
if they sang my name to the wind.
And I doubted *los girasoles*
would understand me anymore,
because now I was speaking
a different language.
I swallowed consonants
and burdened vowels with a sound
so dense, the words fell straight
out of my mouth and hit the ground
before they could reach the river's edge.

I was afraid that, with me gone,
los girasoles would turn away

from the sun and blame the wind
for not bringing me back.
But it would not be the sun's
or the wind's fault;
my parents had uprooted me.

en los estados unidos

En los Estados Unidos
I trained my tongue
and twisted syllables
to form words
that sounded hollow,
like the rain at midnight
dripping into tin pails
through the thatched roof
of our *abuelita*'s house.

En los Estados Unidos
I copied Colonial maps
from a social studies book
with pictures of white men
wearing powdered wigs

and stately white women
in old-fashioned dresses.
Their costumes were never
as colorful as the feathers
of the *matachines* dancing
at sunset in the Christmas parade,
dressed like our Aztec ancestors.

En los Estados Unidos
I nibbled on school lunches
of fish sticks and macaroni
while my soul craved
the chocolaty gravy of mole
on a bed of Spanish rice.

But Mami said we were
the luckiest children because
we had two homes.
Every time we'd get homesick,
we'd gather our belongings
and walk up the street to the bus stop.
The city bus would grumble
and groan as it took us to the edge

of this world.
Then we'd walk the half mile
across the International Bridge
from the border in Eagle Pass
to the *aduana* in Piedras Negras.

The chain-link fence on the bridge
was like a harp, and our fingers
would play a joyful tune upon
its rib cage as we traipsed along,
looking down at the laughing
waters of the Rio Grande
until we reached that other world,
the one we missed so much.

In Piedras Negras
Mami's mother, *mi abuelita* Inez,
was always ready to receive us
at a moment's notice.
When we stayed the night,
she'd roast dry mesquite meal
in an iron skillet
over the coals in her *chimenea*,

then add cinnamon and sugar
to make her special *pinole* for us.
Abuelita would spoon the sweetness
into paper cones.
We loved to hear it whisper
as the loose grains slid up and down
inside our cones, teasing our mouths
as it slipped away from us.

Later we would lie on Abuelita's bed
in her one-room house,
listening to Mami talk about America
and all that she loved about it:
about having children who belonged
to two countries, spoke two languages,
and would someday be at home
on either side.

sisters

One afternoon when I came
home from school, I asked Mami,
"May I go to my *amiguitas*' house?"
Mireya and Sarita, twin sisters
who were both in the fourth grade
with me, were waiting at the gate.

Mami looked at them
through the window and frowned.
"No," she said,
and went back to her sewing.

"But why?" I wailed.
When Mireya and Sarita lingered,
Mami waved them away.

"You want *amiguitas?*" she asked.
"I made you lots of them.
There they are," she declared,
pointing to my five sisters.
"*Cinco hermanitas* for you
to play house with. You want a doll?
This one can be your *muñeca*,"
she said, picking up Rosita.
"She comes with diapers
and a bottle of formula."

"I'm tired of playing *mamá*," I complained.
"You do it. They're *your* kids!"
I sassed her, and for that I had to mop
the entire house, which included
four bedrooms, two bathrooms,
and the kitchen. My *cinco hermanitas*
mocked me from outside
while they dressed up
the baby, Benito, like a girl.

Most days Paco was smart enough
to play alone or with his own friends.

The six of us sisters
were round beads knotted side by side,
like pearls on a necklace,
strung so close together
we always made one another cry.

"If you can't get along," Mami would warn
 through the small kitchen window,
"I'm going to separate you.
Then where will you be,
with no one to play with?"

Six sisters with flashing eyes
as bright as starry nights.
We shared chewed bubble gum
but fought over M&M's.
Analiza, the fierce one, with pretty,
white teeth, would bite down
like a rabid dog and spit out
the bloody taste of sisterly love,
while Tita and Juanita
would pull each other's hair.
Then Rosita would wail like a police siren,

and we'd all be punished.
Six sisters would do penance
in separate closets, teary eyes closed,
praying for someone
we could get along with.

bebés

Even though we didn't always
cherish one another,
Mami had enough *cariño*
for every single one of us.
When we playfully begged to know
which of us was her favorite,
she would tell us
we were all her babies.

For as long as I can remember,
Mami has adored *bebés*.
After all, she kept having them
year after year.
To her, *bebés* are like
pennies from heaven.

The more you have,
the richer you become.

Yet raising so many babies
is expensive. While Papi worked
long hours up in North Texas
building houses
so he and Mami could buy
more formula and diapers,
groceries, school supplies, and clothes,
Mami stayed home with us.
Often Papi was gone for weeks on end.

Every time Mami had a *bebé*,
Papi was happy.
He always went to the bank,
opened up a savings account,
and started a new record book.
Soon there were nine small record books
in Mami's old suitcase,
each one fat with bank receipts
and full of numbers.
One account for Mami and Papi,

because they were as one,
and one for each of us—
for *Quinceañera* parties for the girls'
fifteenth birthdays, for college tuitions,
and for whatever else might come up.

Somehow there has always been
enough to get us through.
Because between the two of them,
Mami and Papi have kept Diosito
pretty busy answering prayers
one shiny penny at a time.

PART THREE

crossing borders

after the storm

Summer after freshman year

The day of Mami's operation
to remove the cancer, Papi and I
sat in the waiting room and
held our breath.

After Mami woke up,
the doctor told us
the surgery had been successful
but she would have to stay
at least six weeks to recover.
Papi quit his job so he could
spend his days with Mami
at the hospital. He says
even after the medical bills,

there's still enough
money in the savings accounts
to pay for everything we need.

Sometimes, while Mami
is lying down, Papi will trace
the arch of her eyebrow
with his fingertips and lean over
to kiss her lips. She is
his Sleeping Beauty.

When she is released
this afternoon, she will have to
come back every other week
for chemotherapy treatments.
On those days Papi will be the one
to bring her and take her home.

But today it's just me here
keeping her company.
Papi's gone to Mexico
to buy her a special gift
we saw at the *mercado*: a blue linen dress

embroidered with dozens of calla lilies,
their white petals folded demurely
as if in prayer, and all around them
hundreds of turtledoves.

"You should be at the mall," Mami says,
"or at the movies with your friends—
not cooped up with me all day.
This is your summer vacation."
She shifts painfully in her bed
and rolls the thermometer around
in her mouth as if it were
a sour lollipop.

"I don't mind. I thought the two of us
could have some fun," I tell her,
pulling her makeup case out of
my backpack. My bag is so old
its leather face is worn and stained,
begging to be retired.
I won't throw it out
because it belonged to Abuelita Inez
when she was young.

Mami eyes the makeup case.
"What's that for?" she asks
as I fluff the pillows behind her.

"Don't you want to look *coqueta* for Papi
when he gets back?" I ask, winking.

"You're so silly!" Mami says,
but she giggles in spite of herself.

Como bandidas, we rifle through
her makeup case. We choose
a lipstick, a small container
of face powder, and blush,
all in soft, subdued colors.
Then she pulls out a tube of mascara
and frowns. She's never liked the stuff.

"It's new," I admit. "I bought it
for your special occasion."

"Having an operation is *not*
a special occasion," she says,

and throws the tube of mascara
back into the case in disgust.

"No," I whisper, kissing her cheek.
"An operation is definitely
  not a special occasion.
  But going home is."

elotes

Piedras Negras, Coahuila, Mexico
Sophomore year

We spent our summer
watching Mami come and go
back and forth from the hospital
in a nauseated haze.
The season slipped by us
undetected and unmourned.
The fact that it's gone
doesn't even matter.

Every Sunday now
Papi, Analiza, Victoria, Paco, and I
cross the border to meet
Abuela Inez at her church,

Nuestra Señora de Guadalupe.
We enter the chapel quietly.
Our eyes adjust to the dimness,
tearing up at the strong scent
of burning incense.
The first thing we do,
even before we sit down,
is stop by the altar
of the Virgen de Guadalupe
to light our candles.
Papi gives each of us a dime,
which we drop into the donation slot
in the metal collection box.

Then we cluster around
Abuela Inez, hold hands,
and pray for Mami together.
Our only requests are
that the chemo treatments
ravaging her body
do not weaken her spirit
and that she can regain herself
when the nightmare is over.

After mass we push open
the heavy wooden doors
of the *iglesia* and step outside.
Squinting at the brightness
of the late September day,
right away we smell
the ears of roasted corn.

Los elotes calientitos—
what Papi calls Mexican gold—
taste better after offering
our hopeful prayers
and leaving church
without the anxiety we felt before.

"How much?" Papi asks,
already unfolding the pressed money
tucked away like starched
handkerchiefs deep in his pockets.
The price is inconsequential.
An American dollar
gets us four ears and change.
We would pay much more.

Los elotes are delicious,
sweating butter and painted
with chili-powdered lime juice.

Analiza and Victoria are too dainty;
they prefer their ears tender,
with pearly baby teeth at the ends.
But not me. I am no wilting violet,
no Spanish rose.
I'm tough, sturdy, and strong.
I want mine like my *papi*'s,
big and firm. Like Paco,
I want to work hard
at that first bite, want my teeth
to press against my gums
as I conquer it:
so good and so spicy,
muy rico y picoso.

las telenovelas

I always cry when I watch
the women, *las mujeres*, suffer
in the *telenovelas*. And they always
suffer. But when they cry,
their mascara doesn't smear,
and they don't look like
raccoons afterward.
Las mujeres in soap operas
always look gorgeous.
They make me feel inadequate,
with my chubby cheeks
and puffy brown eyes.

I glance over at Mami,
sitting beside me on the couch,

her eyes fixed on the screen
while she peels potatoes
into her apron like always.
It's comforting to see
our prayers being answered.
At this moment
no one would guess
Mami's had cancer,
not by the way she carries on
with her normal life.
The pains of summer
are far behind her now.
Since she is no longer in treatment
and never lost her hair,
Mami looks as lovely and
healthy as ever.

People often say I look
just like her. It's true
I have Mami's hair and eyes,
but her skin is different.
Hers is a darker, richer brown.
It gives her a warm glow.

She isn't gorgeous like a movie star,
but she's beautiful.

"Is that going to be you
in a few years, an actress
on TV?" Mami asks,
pointing at the screen
with her potato peeler.

Ever since I became a sophomore
and started taking a drama class,
Mami can't stop talking about
how she's going to sit here
with her *comadres* and watch me
in the *telenovelas* someday.

"Only if I lose about a million
pounds," I answer.

"I was chubby too when I was
your age, but it's just baby fat.
You'll grow out of it," Mami says.
She reaches over and caresses

my face. "You have your father's
fine bone structure. *Hermosa.*"

When she looks at me like this,
I do feel beautiful.
But Mami and I share more
than a resemblance. In the midst
of her busy life, she has carved out
a special time for us.
Every afternoon before dinner,
while the rest of the kids play outside,
she and I become sisters,
agonizing over the unfairness
in the lives of the heroines
of our beloved *telenovelas*.

"It's make-believe!" Papi complains.
He wants to see something real,
like heavyweight boxing.
He paces back and forth in the hall
with his hands in his pockets,
waiting for us, *las dos lloronas*,
to stop wiping our eyes

and leave the living room
so he can watch the fights in peace.

But Mami says, "We can't change
the channel. Lupita's favorite
telenovela is coming on next."

So Papi shakes his head,
takes his cowboy hat off the hook,
and tells us he's leaving
to go drink coffee and talk serious
business with his *compadres*
at the local truck stop.

Mami nudges me.
"*¡Ay, sí!* He wants to watch
those big, beefy guys on television
exchanging blows,
like Muhammed Ali and
George Foreman used to do,"
she whispers. "Nothing more
realistic than that."

drama

"Here you go," says my new
drama teacher, Mr. Cortés,
handing me a smallish white box
and a giant bag of Blow Pops.

At first I don't know
what to make of this
unexpected gift. In drama class
we clown around a lot.
Anything from a spontaneous
Tarzan yell competition
to a pageant on the rooftop
is likely to break out at any time.

"What's this?" I ask.

"Voice lessons," Mr. Cortés declares.
He reaches over, opens the box
with a flourish, and reveals
a set of four instructional CDs.
They're brand-new, still shrink-wrapped.

"Go home and practice the lessons
with these in your mouth," he says,
pointing to the Blow Pops.

He tears into the bag,
and it explodes:
a troupe of colorfully wrapped candy
bounces all around us.
After we pick up
the bubble gum-filled lollipops,
Mr. Cortés unwraps two of them.
He gives them both to me.

"Here, put these in, one on each side
of your mouth, *como ardilla listada*."
He puffs out his cheeks with air
to demonstrate, making a chipmunk face.

"Don't suck on them," he instructs.
"Just let them sit there.
If you're serious about acting—
and I think you are—then you need to
lose your accent."

Rolling the Blow Pops
into position, I wonder if
this is how Mr. Cortés
got rid of his own accent.
The hard candy scrapes
against my gums. My face
is so stretched out, it feels as big as
one of those hot-air balloon characters
floating over the booths
at la Feria, the annual fair
in Piedras Negras.

"Well? Say something,"
Mr. Cortés demands.

I swallow some spit and warble out,
"I have an accent?"

Mr. Cortés doesn't answer me
right away. He's laughing so hard
his shoulders are shaking.
I know I sound ridiculous,
so I can't help but laugh along with him.
When he can finally talk, he teases,
"We're going to need
a lot more Blow Pops."

quinceañera

Today is December 12,
Día de Nuestra Señora de Guadalupe,
the day we celebrate our patron saint,
the Virgin of Guadalupe.
It's also my birthday—
I am fifteen years old.

Mami wakes me up
by singing *"Las mañanitas"*
at my bedside and hugging me so hard,
I think I might burst a lung.

"I'm sorry there is no money
for a *Quinceañera*," she says.
"The chemo . . ."

"I didn't want one," I say,
   interrupting her apology
   because I don't want her to think about
   the expensive treatments
   she had to undergo
   for months after her surgery.

   Besides, I don't want a big fuss,
   a party that's as elaborate
   as a wedding. The idea of wearing
   a frilly dress and tight pantyhose
   makes me shiver,
   but the thought of all those people
   watching me stumble around
   in high-heeled shoes
   while I try to dance
   with some boy I hardly know
   as I am being presented to society
   makes me break out in hives.
   I don't need that kind
   of attention. I'd rather
   stay home and do chores
   than be a pampered debutante.

"Are you sure you don't want
to have a small party and invite
your girlfriends?" Mami asks.

"I'm sure," I tell her. "I just want
to spend time with you guys."

Papi has been working late
at his new job downtown,
building an overpass
with his construction crew.
He's trying to make more money,
to put back into savings
what was spent
on Mami's medical bills.
He comes home every night
covered in so much dirt,
he looks like a blond sand bug.

Mami looks tired all the time,
but she keeps telling us she's fine.
Sitting next to me now,
she studies me seriously for a moment.

Then the brightness comes back
into her eyes,
and she reaches for me.

"Te quiero mucho," Mami says,
wrapping me in her arms so I can feel
just how much she adores me.

señorita

Mami said life would change
after I turned fifteen,
when I became a *señorita*.
But *señorita* means different things
to different people.

For my friends Mireya and Sarita,
who turned fifteen last summer,
señorita means wearing lipstick,
which when I put it on
is sticky and messy,
like strawberry jam on my lips.

For Mami, *señorita* means
making me try on high-heeled shoes

two inches high
and meant to break my neck.

For Mami's sisters, my *tías*
Maritza and Belén, who live in Mexico,
señorita means measuring me,
turning me this way and that
as they fit me for the floral dresses
they cheerfully stitch together
on their sewing machines.
For the aunts, *señorita* also means
insisting I wear pantyhose,
the cruel invention that makes
my thick, trunklike thighs
into bulging sausages.

When my *tías* are done dressing me up
like a big Mexican Barbie doll,
I look at myself in the mirror.
Mami stands behind me
as I pull at the starched
flowered fabric and argue
with Mami's reflection.

"Why do I have to wear this stuff?
This is your style, not mine!
I like jeans and tennis shoes.
Why can't I just dress
like a normal teenager?
En los Estados Unidos, girls
don't dress up like *muñecas*."

"*Señoritas* don't talk back
to their mothers," Mami warns.
When my aunts aren't looking,
she gives me a tiny pinch,
like a bee sting on the inside
of my upper arm. "*Señoritas* know
when to be quiet and let their
elders make the decisions."

For my father, *señorita* means
he has to be a guard dog
when boys are around.
According to my parents,
I won't be allowed to date
until I graduate from high school.

That's fine with me.
I have better things to do
than think about boys—
like prepare for my future.
I want to be the first one in our family
to earn a college degree.

For my sisters, *señorita* means
having someone to worship:
it is the wonder of
seeing their oldest sister
looking like Cinderella
on her way to the ball.

But for me, *señorita* means
melancolía: settling into sadness.
It is the end of wild laughter.
The end of chewing bubble gum
and giggling over nothing
with my friends at the movies, our feet up
on the backs of the theater seats.

Señorita is very boring
when we go to a fancy restaurant

decorated with Christmas lights
for the upcoming *Posadas.*
We sit properly, Papi, Mami,
and I, quietly celebrating
my fifteenth birthday
with due etiquette because
I'm trying my best
to be a good daughter and accept
the clipping of my wings,
the taming of my heart.

Being a *señorita*
is not as much fun
as I'd expected it to be.
It means composure and dignity.

Señorita is a *niña,*
the girl I used to be,
who has lost her voice.

to be or not to be mexican

"Anyone want my enchi-lady?"
Sarita says, picking up an enchilada
with her fork and showing it to
a group of our friends
who are sitting with us in the cafeteria.

I shake my head
and take a bite of my burrito.
When I look up again,
everyone around me is laughing,
but I don't get the joke.

Sarita's enchilada just hangs limply
over her fork, looking soggy

in its coat of red sauce,
like a big, overcooked noodle.
What's so funny about that?

Sarita glances at me sideways,
holds up a taco, and says,
"How about a tay-co?
Anyone want a tay-co?"

Again the table erupts in laughter.
I look around. As usual,
the freshmen table is quiet.
And the sophomores, who sit behind us,
always look lost.
But not us. No—we're juniors,
and we're loud.
Every day, the cafeteria
walls shake with our laughter.

"Why are you talking like that?" I ask.

"Like what? Like you?" Sarita smirks.
She licks her index finger and strikes

the air as if she's just scored
a point against me.

"I don't talk like that," I protest.

"Yes, you do," Mireya jumps in.
"You talk like you're one of *them*."
She spits out the word in disgust
and looks down at her lunch tray,
like she can't stand the sight of me.

"One of *them*?" I ask.

"Let me translate for you,"
Sarita sneers. "You talk like
you wanna be white."

The girls around us
aren't laughing so much anymore.
They're all eyes now,
hoping for a food fight.
Mosquitas muertas, two-faced
flies on the wall.

"What," Sarita asks, "you think you're
Anglo now 'cause you're in Drama?
You think you're better than us?"

"No—"

"Then stop trying to act like
them," Mireya says accusingly.
"You're Mexican, just like the rest of us.
Look around you. Ninety-nine percent
of this school is Mexican.
Stop trying to be something you're not!"

With that, both sisters
pick up their trays and walk away.
They don't even give me
a chance to respond.
The other girls follow them,
a convoy of high-heeled hyenas
in mass migration.

Suddenly I feel familiar arms around me
and hear Victoria's voice in my ear.

She must have seen what happened
from her seat at the freshmen table.

"Don't listen to them, *manita*," my sister
whispers. "They're just jealous."

"Jealous of what?" I ask.

"I don't know. Your acting?
Maybe they think
you don't want to be part
of their group anymore."

"Just because of how I talk?"
I ask heatedly. "What—
because I'm Mexican
I'm supposed to speak with an accent?
Should I wear a *rebozo* too?"
I think of Abuela Inez
wearing her embroidered white
shawl wrapped around her head
and draped over her shoulders
everywhere she goes.

"Being Mexican
means more than that.
It means being there for each other.
It's togetherness, like a *familia*.
We should be helping one another,
cheering our friends on, not trying
to bring them down."

Victoria holds me tight
while I suck in my breath,
stifling the urge to scream.

I'm not acting white! I want to shout
after my so-called friends.
*I couldn't be more Mexican
if you stamped a cactus on my forehead.*

swimming
the rio grande

San Vicente, Coahuila, Mexico

It is Sunday
and the sun
is an Aztec god
so powerful
you can go blind
if you stare at it too long.

After so many months
of anxiety and stress,
it is a blessing
to be on spring break;
to feel at home again
in Mexico;

to float on our backs,
close our eyes,
and just relax
while Mami sits
on a blanket and watches us
from the riverbank
with her eagle eyes.

Papi is stranded
in the shade
of the mesquite trees
because he is *güero*,
not dark like we are,
and the sun god
has turned him red
like a boiled crawfish.

As for me, today
I am a bronzed mermaid,
weightless and swift.
My hair floats before me
like seaweed
as I pierce the golden

surface of the river
and come up for air.

Paco is a predator,
swimming underwater,
trying to scare us
by nipping at our toes
with a clothespin.
His shark belly
is big and swollen
with warm river water
and cold hot dogs
that he snuck
out of the ice chest
when Mami wasn't looking.

Analiza and Victoria
are water sprites,
diving for pretty rocks
and collecting them
in the socks they'd been
wearing—*calcetines* that were
Sunday school white

this morning
but are now dingy
and stretched out
enough to fit Bigfoot.

Come Monday morning
Mami will shake her head
and say *"¡Ay, chihuahua!"*
as she pulls the *calcetines*
over her knuckles
and scrubs them hard
against each other.

For now we are frogs
bobbing up and down
and side to side
with our eyes half closed,
letting the sun,
our Ancient Father,
the patron god of our ancestors,
kiss our naked foreheads
from far up in the sky.

the notebook

I'm always the last one
to leave the classroom
at the end of the day.
I don't like the pushing
and shoving, or the loud,
boisterous roughhousing
that goes on while everyone
is trying to get out of school
at the same time
as if they're escaping
from Alcatraz.
I like to sit back and let
everyone else go by.
Then I can actually breathe
when I walk the halls.

Today, after the final bell rings,
while I'm waiting
for the rush to subside,
Mireya and Sarita
walk past my desk.
Without saying a word,
Mireya hands me my blue
composition notebook,
the one in which I write
all my secrets, everything
I'm feeling inside.

Noticing the puzzled look
on my face, Sarita says,
"You left it in gym class, genius,"
before she turns
and follows her sister
out the doorway.

I walk home in silence,
gripping that blue notebook
close to my heart,
kicking myself

for having left it unguarded
and hoping Mireya hasn't read
any of my private thoughts—
especially my poetry.

But as I sit alone
in my bedroom
flipping through the pages
of familiar verse,
I see that she has.
My heart becomes a butterfly
trapped in a glass jar, beating
its wings wildly in my chest,
when I realize that she's put
a small, pink sticky note
on the poem I wrote
about that day in the cafeteria.

The note is strategically placed
next to the stanza
in which I described how
"all the girls around me
dropped their scarlet

mouths wide-open, like a circle
of Venus flytraps, and laughed
hysterically at me."

In Mireya's distinct, quiet
handwriting there are only
two words: "I'm sorry."

on the way

With the competition season
just beginning, the buzz at school
has been all about UIL.
Every year, across the state,
students vie for top places
in the academic, athletic,
and performing arts categories,
hoping for a chance to advance
to the next level.

Riding the bus home
from the District meet,
Mireya leans over my seat
and looks down at me resting
on my back, cradling a tall,
shiny trophy in my arms.

I still can't believe it: I won
top place in Poetry Interpretation
for my dramatic performance
of the poem "The Highwayman."
In Ready Writing, my essay
earned fifth place—but
that doesn't mean as much
to me. Writing has always come easily.
Acting, however, is a newfound
passion—and a trophy
is the Holy Grail of awards,
far more elusive
than a standard ribbon.
You can try your best
all through high school
and never win a trophy in anything.

Mireya and Sarita didn't place
in their events, Science and Math.
They've been keeping
their empty hands busy,
absently paging through magazines.

"You still mad at me?" Mireya asks.

"No," I answer, and look away.
It's the first time
she's actually talked to me
since the incident in the cafeteria.

"It's a cool trophy," Mireya says,
reaching down
to caress it with reverence.

"Thanks. I love it," I whisper,
hugging it to my chest. It's my first
competition ever, and I can't wait
to show the trophy to Mami.

"I guess it was worth it,
changing the way you talk,"
Mireya admits. Her smile
is soft, sincere.

Suddenly I hear Mr. Cortés,
at the front of the bus,
laughing about something
with another teacher.

I look up at Mireya.
"Changing how I talk
  doesn't change who I am.
  I know where I came from," I tell her,
  and she nods.

Mireya and I have been in school
together since first grade,
two chicks cooped up in the same pen,
pecking at each other,
sometimes a little too hard.
We've been best friends
for as long as I can remember.
I guess a little drama
is just what we needed
to remind us that while friends
are the *familia* we choose
for ourselves, we still have to work
at staying close.

a moment
in the spotlight

When I walk into the house
holding my trophy proudly
before me, Mami screams,
leaps off the couch, and hops around
like a Mexican jumping bean.
You'd think she had just won
the lottery. She hugs me, rocks
me, kisses me. It's just
ridiculous how happy she is.

"Look at my beautiful, talented
muchachita," she keeps telling Papi.

"Ah, she is not so little anymore,"
Papi says to Mami

as he stands beside me,
smiling proudly.

Victoria sits wearily on the couch.
She's already touched the trophy
enough times on the bus.
All she wants now
is to get some sleep.
But Analiza and the others
crowd around to admire
what I've won as Mami holds it
in her arms. Even Benito
takes his finger out of his mouth
long enough to point at the trophy,
his eyes as big and round as buttons.

"Can you believe it?" I ask Mami,
watching her wipe away happy tears.

"Of course I can," she replies.
"You're a rising star,
the light on our horizon."

PART FOUR

give us this day

news

Junior year

When Papi gives us the news
at the breakfast table,
Analiza and Victoria
stare at him wide-eyed.
It's been a year and a half
since Mami had her last
chemotherapy treatment,
and although most of Papi's
money has been spent
on the hope of saving her life,
the cancer has returned.

"But I thought she was okay,"
I whisper, fighting
not to lose it in front of them.

"Well, even with chemotherapy,
there's never a guarantee
the cancer won't come back,"
Papi explains quietly.
"I guess, in your *mami*'s case,
it did. She'll just have to
have more chemo."

I hang my head, a weeping
willow, my long hair shading me
from their sight. Papi gets up,
gathers all three of us in his arms,
and tries to share his strength with us;
but I can feel him shaking
as I hide my face in his chest.

Within a week, *tías* and *tíos*,
family friends, neighbors,
nuns, and even social workers
begin to come by our house.
They talk in low voices and look at us
with watery, sympathetic eyes.
But at the end of each day

we are left alone
with our unspoken fears:
eight kids huddled together
in one bedroom, praying,
begging for Mami's *salud*
to be restored.

Cancer has more than
invaded our home.
It has closed the doors
behind itself, drawn the curtains,
and locked us in for good.

mami's roses

Even though the second round
of chemo treatments
is weakening her,
Mami keeps tending her garden.
Another spring has arrived,
and there are many roses now,
sitting prettily under the high
canopy of the tall mesquite:
white ones, yellow ones, red ones,
even a mauve one that she's afraid
she might never see bloom again.

Mami loves her roses
almost as much as she loves us.
She sings to them every morning

in her polyester shorts
like a free-spirited hippie
with a scarf tied around her hair.
She walks around the garden,
bending here and there,
testing the soil,
and pulling out young weeds
with her bare hands.

"How do you get your roses
to bloom so much?"
her *comadres* ask.

Mami smiles generously
and tells them her secret:
she pinches off the excess buds
so that only one rose
blooms on each stem.
She says it's better this way;
when too many roses
feed off the same stem,
they are not very healthy
because they take one another's food.

That philosophy
hardly seems like her.
Mami's cultivating six budding
daughters and two rowdy sons:
eight thriving blue roses
clustered together
so closely, they tremble
as they cling to the withering
stem of her waning life.

the actress

I come out of the bathroom,
and Mami is sitting on my bed,
weeping. In her pink nightgown,
she looks slim and fragile.

"Why were you crying and talking
to yourself in there?" she demands,
her voice quivering.
"Tell me what you were saying."

"I wasn't really crying," I explain.
"I was practicing my part
in *The Trojan Women*, playing out a scene
between Hecuba and Andromache
after the fall of Troy. It's called a solo.
I have to perform it for drama class."

She looks at me in sudden wonder.
"Do it. Speak the English," she begs.
Even though she is forty-two years old,
Spanish is the only language she speaks.
It just isn't necessary to learn English
in our small, bilingual town.
But now, though she won't understand
the English, she wants to experience the piece
the way I've been practicing it at school.

"Okay," I say nervously.
I've never performed for Mami.
Up to this point, all my acting
has taken place in class with Mr. Cortés
or in front of the judges at competitions.

I slip into the bathroom again
and take two towels from the shelf.
Back in my room, standing before Mami,
I improvise, cradling the towels in my arms
as if they were baby Astyanax's
tiny corpse. My performance goes
from melancholy to desperate
to angry—and with the final words

I go down on my knees
like a felled tree. Mami cries
through the whole thing.

Afterward, sitting on the floor,
leaning my back against her knees,
I tell Mami about my role in the play.
She devours every word as I recount
the field trips, the exhilaration
and the intensity of competition.
I describe the Trojan women characters,
and she makes me translate their words
as she combs my hair.

"*¡Qué talento!*" she exclaims,
  kissing the crown of my head.
"So gifted to be able to put
  yourself in their place!"

I don't tell her that this is how
  I've dealt with the last two years
  of seeing her suffer.

what's gone

I used to look forward to
the weekend the way I looked forward
to spring. Now one day
is the same as the next.
Outside, everything is green
and full of life, which makes
everything inside our house
that much more depressing.

Pretending to nap beside Mami,
through one open eye I watch Papi,
who is sitting on the edge of the bed.
He leafs through the record books
of accounts that are as empty
as our refrigerator.
Then he hangs his head and cries.

I want to throw back the covers,
run to him, and put my arms
around him. But one thing holds me
back: I don't know how
he will react. He is not the same Papi
that he was before the cancer
took over our lives.

Sometimes his change of mood
is as surprising as
a sudden shift in the direction
of billowing smoke.
I know he wouldn't purposely
hurt me; he's just venting
his frustrations.
So when I feel his anger
blowing my way,
I hold my breath
and try to see through it.
But then the smoke burns my eyes
till they start to water,
and I know it's time to move—
find a clear spot
away from the smoldering coals.

Most times, though,
his anger is nothing more
than a change of weather—
a blistering breeze,
a pool that's cooled—
and he doesn't want to talk
to anyone about it.
So now, not knowing
which face of sadness
he might show, I play it safe
and leave him alone.

Later, in the kitchen, I discover
all nine of our record books
stuffed into the garbage can.
When Papi finds me standing there
fishing them out
with tears running down my face,
he pulls the books
out of my fierce grip,
throws them back in the trash,
and hugs me tight.

"Money is inconsequential," he says,
proudly straightening himself
before he continues. "We don't need
to hold on to these anymore.
What's gone is gone."

a simple plan

"What is there to think about?
Mami needs this," I tell Papi,
sitting across from him
at our worn kitchen table.
I'm finishing my homework.
He's paying bills again
and thumbing through a brochure
of a cancer clinic in Galveston, Texas.

"I know," he says,
nodding without looking at me.
"And this place is special.
They have the best medical staff
in the country, and they also have
psychiatric and spiritual programs.

This is everything she needs
and so much more.
I just don't know
how we're going to do it."

"It's so simple," I tell Papi
as I close my notebook.

"Simple?" Papi repeats.
He looks at me skeptically.
Then he pushes
his chair back, gets up,
and starts pacing the room
with his hands in his pockets.

"*Sí,*" I answer,
playing with my pencil.
"While Mami is in Galveston
getting her chemo,
you can work closer to her,
in Houston. I'll stay here
and take care of the kids.
That way you can go see her

every day at the clinic
and just come home on weekends
to check on us."

"I don't know," he says,
biting the inside of his cheek
as he mulls it over.

"Papi. I'm a junior
in high school, almost
an adult. I can handle it.
Besides, it's May already.
School will be out soon.
It won't be so bad—
just three months."

"Just three months, huh?
Sure, no problem,"
Papi says sarcastically.
"Like pouring a truckload
of wet concrete
through a six-inch sieve."

mother, may I

Summer after junior year

June is here, and Papi
is with Mami in Galveston,
more than six hours away.
Although it was hard
to convince him at first,
Papi finally listened to reason
and left me in charge.

"Mother, may I?"
        "Mother, may I?"

My wayward sister
Analiza taunts me
as she runs away from me,

opens the gate, and takes off
for a friend's house
to talk to boys on the phone.
"Come back here!" I scream.
"You have dishes to wash."

"You have dishes to wash!"
Paco parrots as he clips
his toenails on the porch.

"Don't do that out here.
Get inside!" I holler, but he just
shoves his stinky foot in my face
and laughs at me.

While the little ones
ignore their chores,
race down the street, climb trees,
and look for *chicharras*
trilling in the mesquites,
Victoria stays behind
and helps me mop the floors.
She's my only ally.

Mami made it look so easy,
raising kids—"like pruning roses,"
she used to say.
But most days it feels like
the current of the Rio Grande
is swallowing us up.

Analiza has started wearing
makeup. She knows
Mami wouldn't allow it—
she won't turn fifteen
for two more months—
but I can't get her to stop.
Paco claims she even
has a boyfriend.

I pray every day for a miracle,
or for the legendary la Llorona,
that horrifying ghost
of a mother, to carry off
my troublemaking siblings
when she collects the souls
of other misbehaving children.

making tortillas

I don't know how she did it—
how Mami was always able to rise
before the birth of light
and shape row upon row
of beautifully molded *testales*,
which would become tortillas;
how she breathed life into
the balls of dough and placed them
gently, like baby chicks,
into a nest of dishtowels
before she rushed to begin her day.

Nothing bothered her
when she was making tortillas.
Not even Benito,

knifed painfully on her hip,
could make her lose her concentration.
She was always focused
as she took out her rolling pin
and dusted a board with flour,
then rolled the fleshy spheres of dough
into powdered, flat circles
as perfectly round as
a full moon beaming outside
her kitchen window before dawn.

In the afternoon, as *merienda*,
an after-school snack, she made
another two and a half dozen tortillas
while she warmed a bottle for the *nene*
and sang a romantic ballad *en español*
to the older ones, who sat
wide-eyed at the table.

At night the same ritual again.
The television roaring,
the girls fighting, Paco bellyaching,
Papi snoring on the couch,

and Mami calmly wiping
the sweat off her brow
with her rolled-up sleeves as she stood
at the kitchen counter
pounding away at the soft dough
stretched out complacently before her,
a smile illuminating her face.

a mesquite
in the rose garden

In the squint of morning,
before anyone else is awake,
when the roaring sounds
of unbridled verses
rush furiously through my head,
the mesquite is my confidant.
I lean back against its sturdy trunk
and read aloud every word
imprinted *en mi corazón*.
The mesquite listens quietly—
as if the poems budding in my heart,
then blossoming in my notebook,
are Scripture—and never tells a soul
the things I write.

pomegranates, perch, and roasted doves

This morning, at breakfast time,
the little ones were crying.
They wanted something to eat,
and I had nothing to give them.
We ran out of food
during the week,
and only the free lunches
at school sustain us.

But the knots writhing
in my own stomach
are not from hunger.
Worry feeds me
with a festering spoon;

the meals are enough
to make me want to vomit.

Mami is still at the clinic
in Galveston.
Papi has not come home
in weeks. He's never been gone
this long before.
I can hear the distance in his voice
when he calls. At Mami's side,
he is all but lost to us.
The resolve to save her
consumes him.

This afternoon as Paco
walked out the back door,
I called to him.
He is fourteen now,
with a mind of his own.
I don't want him to become
un vago wandering the streets
and make Mami's worst fears
come to life.

"Hey, *¿adónde vas?*"
  I asked him anxiously.

"Out. With my friends,"
  he answered as he jumped over
  the fence, defying the gate
  I had locked this morning.

"Judas!" I screamed
  as I watched him meet his friends
  at the end of the alley.
"When are you coming back?"
  I yelled, but he ignored me.

So I sat under the mesquite,
  devouring my fingernails,
  crying. Benito sat beside me,
  flipping through my English book,
  pointing at the pictures
  with his chubby finger—
  Emily Dickinson,
  William Shakespeare,

Edgar Allan Poe—old friends
who offered no consolation.

This evening I managed to get
the little ones to bed early.
The cool evening breeze
and my off-key rendition
of "*Los tres cochinitos*"
had just lulled them to sleep
when suddenly I heard
Paco and his friends
making a commotion
in the darkened kitchen.
They were laughing
as they took the top shelf
out of the refrigerator.

"We're making dinner,"
they announced,
and I followed them outside.
They built a fire pit
out of old cinder blocks

and placed the wire shelf over it
to use as a grill.
Then my brother showed me
his treasure: a sack of pomegranates,
the dappled, dull red fruit
hiding plump jewels inside;
a five-gallon bucket
filled with perch, their silver scales
shimmering as they squirmed;
and a bagful of still, gray turtledoves,
their breast feathers
fluttering lifelessly in the breeze.

Now, after peeling
and cleaning and cooking,
here we are—
all eight of us
plus Paco's friends—
awake and sitting by a roaring fire,
feasting at midnight.
Paco is playing the harmonica,
the little ones giggle
when we tickle them,

and everyone is smiling.
The doves are tender,
the perch, flaky, delicious.
And the pomegranates,
like memories, are bittersweet
as we huddle together,
remembering just how good
life used to be.

ice cream from heaven

Two weeks ago Papi's
oldest brother, Tío Saúl,
his wife, and their son
showed up at our house
bearing gifts, their pickup truck
full of groceries. But now
all that food is gone.

Yesterday Serafina
came over to talk like she used to
when Mami was home.
We sat at the kitchen table
and drank *limonada*,
watching over the usual chaos
while the kids wove their way

around us, holding hands
in a chain, making serpentine
twists and turns as they played
their favorite sing-along game,
La víbora de la mar.

"You're doing a good job, Lupita,"
Serafina said, patting my hand.
"But don't forget to have fun.
I can always babysit if you want
to go out with your friends."

After she went back home,
she sent her son over with
some ground beef and a bag of rice.
We didn't have anything
left in the cupboards
to cook with it, so Victoria and I
sent the little ones out
to ask for food again.

Rosita borrowed two tomatoes
from Mami's *comadre* Lucía.

Juanita got an onion
and two cloves of garlic
from a friend of hers
who snuck them out of the kitchen
without asking permission
because her mother is tired
of "lending" us food.

Tita didn't want to go begging;
she's too shy. So we made do
with what we got.
Victoria cooked some Spanish rice,
and I made a meat casserole
with a beautiful zucchini,
a gift from our neighbor
Doña Pepita, who is always
coming over to check on us.

This is how, with Mami and Papi
gone all summer, we've managed
to survive—by our wits
and the generosity
of family and friends.

For the most part, everyone
has been patient and kind.

But this morning I know
God was really watching.
A dairy truck
fat with merchandise
heaved a great sigh and died
right in front of Paco
and his two *amigos*,
who were playing catch
on the sidewalk
at the end of the block.

The driver told the boys
that by the time a mechanic
could come out to fix his truck
the ice cream would melt.
He said they could take it
if they had room
in their freezers at home.
Paco assured him
ours was empty.

When he came in
hauling all those drippy, wet
cartons of ice cream
in a trash bag, I sent
the little ones down there
to get as much
as they could carry
in their skinny arms.
Analiza followed them;
and like a trail of tiny ants,
they came home loaded.

I called Mireya and Sarita,
and they came over.
We sat out on the porch, talking
and laughing all afternoon.
We caught up
on all the *chisme*
and ate ice cream till
we thought we'd burst.

So far today we've had
ice cream sandwiches

and Rocket Pops,
frozen yogurt
and Fruit Squirts.
But we're all in agreement:
there's nothing better than
Neapolitan for dinner
and Rocky Road
for dessert.

PART FIVE

cut like a diamond

mami's home

Senior year

It's late in August when Mami
finally gets to come home.
Papi carries her inside like a child.
Her arms around his neck are
as thin as the delicate trumpet vines
that cling to the trellis
outside my window.
Mami, who once cradled
toddlers in her strong arms,
is now slight and frail—
even more than she was
before she left for Galveston.
When Papi tucks her into bed,
she who once held the stars captive

in her eyes looks up at us
from between her sheets
as if she doesn't recognize us anymore.

We crowd around her
like baby chicks eager
for the warmth under her wing.
Victoria shows Mami the script
for a dramatic duet she and I
are working on for UIL
now that Victoria's also in Drama.
But after a moment Papi
ushers Victoria and the others
out of the room. I stay behind,
holding Mami's trembling hand in mine.

"Look at it, all grown up," says Mami,
mesmerized by the sight of
the mesquite swaying sensually
outside the bedroom window.
With heavy pruning and much-needed
guidance, the tree has become
a graceful and imposing presence

in Mami's beloved rose garden.
"Who'd have known it would be
so beautiful," she marvels.

I agree, but it isn't its beauty
that strikes me. I envy the mesquite
its undaunted spirit, its ability to turn
even a disabling pruning
into an unexpected opportunity
to veer in a different direction,
flourishing more profusely than before.

Papi tries to send me away
from Mami's bedside. He reminds her
that she needs to rest to get better.
Mami says she wants him
to drive us all to San Vicente
this weekend—take us back
to the river and the ranch,
where we can have a good time—
give us back our childhood.

good-bye to mexico

San Vicente, Coahuila, Mexico

Growing up *en los Estados Unidos,*
every weekend we were
more than eager to escape
the suburban world of El Águila
to indulge in the simple pleasures
of Papi's rural hometown
across the border, where we
were true Mexicans, for a day.

Analiza, Victoria, and I
would throw all the kids' belongings
into the bed of Papi's truck
before the first breath of dawn
on Saturday mornings.

The drive took more than an hour.
The younger kids usually
squeezed up front with Papi
while the rest of us
sat jumbled together
in the back of the pickup.
Our legs and arms tossed carelessly
over frayed backpacks,
worn sleeping bags, and pillows,
we would collide against one another
as the old blue Ford
made its way down the *carretera*,
then hit the unpaved roads
through the woods leading
to San Vicente.

But this Saturday
is different. It's been a long time
since we've come
for an ordinary weekend visit.
So much has changed for us
between now and the last time
we drove down.

As we near Tío Rodrigo's
ranch house, I look up
at the treetops.
The morning is dark,
and the moon in this place
is wearing a pale, thin dress
as it seems to jump from behind
one cloud to another, hiding
its exquisite face from us.
I spot the malevolent Lechuza,
the hooting, gray Ghost Owl,
perched on a bony tree limb.
She seems to cast a spell on us
before gliding silently away
on magical wings
the color of moon dust.
The gnarled *huisaches*,
the mesquite's wilder,
wicked cousins, scratch
the sides of Papi's pickup truck.
The branches' thorny ends
are long fingernails
tearing at our hair.

When we arrive,
Papi pulls down the tailgate
and lets us out.
We have finally come back
to play with our cousins:
Gabriela, Tío Rodrigo's
oldest daughter, who is
only two months older than me;
and her two younger sisters,
girls like Raggedy Ann dolls
with unblinking eyes,
hollow cheekbones,
and dry, thin mouths
sewn shut by hunger.

The grown-ups pull Papi inside
to catch him up on the news
while all the younger kids,
a throng of boisterous cousins,
run down to the corral
to watch the *vaqueros*
break in a new herd
of wild horses.

As Gabriela and I pair up
and start off on the trail
to walk the goats to the river,
I start to relax a little.
Here, the weekend actually
feels like a weekend.
I am slowly shifting gears,
adjusting to the rough terrain.
My body takes every dip and turn
of a gulch as awkwardly
as a wobbly wagon wheel,
and I laugh nervously
every time I lose my footing.
But I am glad to be here,
listening to Gabriela's lyrical voice
and the tinkling bells
tied to the necks of the billy goats
that are milling around us,
licking the dew off
spare blades of slender grass
while Gabriela and I
drink black coffee
from the cold lip

of a spotted tin cup.
We worry aloud about Mami,
who is at home
being cared for by her sisters,
Tía Maritza and Tía Belén.

On our way back
from the river,
I jump at the warning rattle
of *cascabeles* in the brush.
For a second
I would almost rather
be back in El Águila,
with the sound of cars honking
in its narrow streets.

In the afternoon, though,
I am happy to join
an impromptu game of volleyball
over a sagging net set up
in the school playground
next to San Vicente's main well.
Gabriela, her two school friends,

and I—an all-girl team
assembled at the last minute—
play against a pack
of teenage boys
whose bare chests glisten,
dark as old pennies.
Their native eyes
are fiercely narrowed
at me, the outsider—
but I am thrilled to be playing;
and when I score a point,
their wide lips grow
into approving smiles
that make me blush.

After the game I miss
the conveniences of home
as Gabriela, her friends, and I
walk carefully along the path
that leads us down
a precarious cliff
to wash our hair
in the chilled waters

of an *ojito*. The creek
runs crookedly
toward the Rio Grande,
the river of memories
that separates me
from the luxury
of indoor plumbing.

In the evening
Papi sleeps on a hammock
in the front yard
while my siblings and I
lie on top of
sleeping bags and pillows
on the bed of our truck,
underneath the cover
of a darkened sky,
listening to the drone of crickets
and the faint snap of fireflies.
Come morning we'll be
on the road, driving
back to El Águila.
So we stay up all night

reliving our adventures
in San Vicente,
remembering when Mami
used to join us—wondering
if she ever will again—
and waiting for the sunrise,
hoping it will chase away
the feeling of *melancolía*
that overwhelms us
as we prepare to say good-bye
to Mexico.

apparition

Late at night, rolling thunder
shakes our house.
When I get up to close
the windows, I find Mami
sitting on the couch
alone in the living room,
sobbing in the dark.
She is so upset,
I can't console her.

Analiza wakes up
and comes in to join us.
Flashes of lightning
give us distorted glimpses
of the terror in Mami's eyes.

We stand on either side of her,
holding her hands
and stroking her thinned hair,
telling her everything's
going to be all right.
But when Mami tells us why
she's crying, Analiza panics
and runs to get Papi.

A moment later
Papi walks softly into the room.
He sits down next to Mami,
puts his arms around her,
and asks, "What's wrong?"

"She saw a ghost!" Analiza exclaims.

"Shut up," I hiss. Her words
freeze the blood in my veins.
I cross myself
from my forehead
down to my heart
and back across my chest.

"I saw her! La Muerte!" Mami wails
  as she clings to my father.

"What?" Papi asks her incredulously.

"The skeleton of death
  coming down the street.
  Dressed like a bride," Mami says.
"She stopped in front of the gate
  and turned to look at our home.
  I can still hear her
  clicking her teeth at me.
  It was horrible!"

"Hush now," Papi tells her gently.
"There's no such thing."
  And just to make sure,
  he pulls back the curtains
  and looks outside. "See?
  There's no one out there."

But Mami is adamant.
"A man dressed in black

came running after la Muerte.
He caught up to her at the gate,
and they went off together."

"It was probably just
  some teenagers," Papi concludes,
"coming home late
  from a dance or a party."

"No, no," Mami insists,
  weeping uncontrollably.
"La Muerte is coming for me.
  She knows where I live."

the natural

"I don't understand why
you're giving up like this.
Where's your gumption, your passion?"
Mr. Cortés lectures me,
standing over my desk.
After the first reading of the script
for the spring play,
he told me to see him after class.
From where I sit I can see kids
hurrying down the hall,
trying to catch their buses home.

When he asks me what's going on,
I shrug my shoulders.

It's no use trying. The fight's
gone out of me.

"You're a senior now, Lupita.
You have all this experience,
and yet you're not using it,"
Mr. Cortés continues.
"This is your time to shine!"
He rolls up a script
like a big, fat burrito and gives me
a friendly smack on the head
to snap me out of my funk.

"I can't," I say flatly,
trying to hand my script back to him.
"You're just going to have to find
someone else for the part."

"That's the problem," Mr. Cortés says,
placing the script purposefully
on my desk. "You're the only one
here who can cry on cue.
You're a natural."

"You think I'm a natural?"
Suddenly my voice breaks.
"I'm not faking it, Mr. Cortés.
My life's a nightmare—that's
why I can cry when I act."

Tears run down my cheeks
without my permission,
leaving hot trails on my face
like rivulets of melting wax
from a candle burned much too long.
But I don't want to hide my feelings
anymore. I'm tired of acting,
tired of pretending
that everything's all right
when it's not.

"Lupita, what's wrong?"
Mr. Cortés asks gently,
eyes filled with concern
as he pulls up a desk
and sits down facing me.
"Is it something at home?"

"Everything's wrong," I say,
wiping my eyes with the back
of my hand. "My mom's sick,
and she's not going to get better."

I wasn't planning to tell him
about Mami, but once I start,
the words stampede out of me,
a herd of untamed horses
breaking out of an unstable corral.

"She's been through
all the cancer treatments," I say.
"There really isn't
anything else they can do."

Mr. Cortés reaches for
the box of tissues on his desk
and holds it out to me.
"I'm so sorry, Lupita. I had no idea."

I nod and blow my nose
before going on.

"Now she just lies there moaning
    all night. It scares the little ones,
    so they crawl into bed with me.
    I can hardly sleep.
    It's gotten so bad,
    this morning I told my dad
    he should call 911.
    We got into a fight about it.
    I told him it's better for Mami
    to die in a hospital
    than for my brothers and sisters
    to remember her like this
    for the rest of their lives."

Mr. Cortés is quiet for a minute.
    Then he asks, "What did your father say
    about taking her to the hospital?"

"He said he can't," I choke out.
    "I'm scared to think about her dying.
    I don't even want her to go
    to the hospital. I just want
    everything to be the way it was."

"Of course you do."
 Mr. Cortés puts his hand on my arm.
"I can't imagine what it must be like
 for you. But I know
 you'll make it through.
 You've come so far.
 Don't shut down now.
 Maybe you could take
 that pain, that energy, and use it
 to become someone else for a while.
 It won't change what's happening
 at home, but it might
 help you cope with it."

I know he's right. This is what
I've been doing all along.
Acting has been my life raft.

I stare at a graduation announcement
posted on the wall, dreading
the possibility of Mami not being there
to share that special day,
and so many more to come.

Suddenly I realize
how much I can't control, how much
I am not promised.
The thought of it
hits me broadside. More tears
squeeze out. I wipe them away.

Mr. Cortés breaks into my thoughts.
"You have a gift, Lupita.
True performers are able to turn
their most painful experiences
into art that other people
can connect with.
You do this exceptionally well.
I think you should take the part."

"I'll think about it," I say.

Mr. Cortés smiles.
"Take your time. Read the script.
Don't forget about what I said.
And remember," he adds,
"I'm here if you need to talk."

I pick up the script again
and thank him on my way out,
knowing no matter what happens,
onstage or off,
the show must go on.

at the hospital

My script lies curled up
beside the neglected bowl
of broth on Mami's food tray.
This time two years ago,
during spring break, our family
was splashing in the Rio Grande,
obliviously happy.

A world away
from San Vicente now,
instead of learning my lines
for my role in the school play,
I sit listening to the raindrops
beating themselves against
the cold windowpanes

as Mami drifts in and out
of a medicated fog.

She asks for her mother often.
I lie and tell Mami she came,
but she had to go back to Mexico
because her visitor's pass
was only good for one day.
I don't have the heart to tell her
Abuela Inez says
she doesn't like hospitals
and just won't come.

Mami believes me
and closes her eyes again
with that awful frown etched
permanently on her forehead.
I want to wipe the crease
from her brow—and the pain
that causes it—to restore the calm,
natural beauty of her face,
so I push gently at her skin
with my fingertips
while she sleeps.

Earlier today Mireya came by
and stayed for a few hours.
She brought me a new journal
and chocolates in a ribboned box.
We didn't get to talk much,
but she said she'd be back.

Papi comes to visit Mami every day,
brings me food, and tells me
I need to take a break
and go home for a while.
But something in me can't
let go of her, the tug
of my old umbilical cord
still strong between us.

Mami wakes up when
Papi comes in. She begs him
to take good care of us,
and I watch him grip the metal bar
on her hospital bed—
the skin on the back of his hands
is taut; his knuckles are marbles—
as he twists himself into a knot.

After a moment
I cross the room to stand beside
Papi and rub his back.

Waiting for la Muerte to take Mami
is like being bound,
lying face up on the sacrificial altar
of the god Huitzilopochtli,
pleading with the Aztec priest,
asking him to be kind
while he rips out my heart.

a night to remember

Days ago Papi took over
the vigil at the hospital.
Now I'm doing my best
to hold myself together
while I get back to the routine
of life at school.

In the middle of the night,
Victoria and I lie in the dark
and whisper comforting words
to each other.
Because we can't sleep,
eventually we get up to practice
our dramatic duet.
Next month we will compete

in the UIL District meet.
We are as nervous
as butterflies unfolding
their wings, preparing
for their first flight.
Everyone at school is expecting us
to take first place.

There's nothing more frustrating
than having your favorite sister
as your duet partner.
We spend most of our time
snapping at each other,
perfecting our performance,
critiquing every word,
one sharp sting at a time.

But tonight when we finally
get it right, we celebrate
as only unattended *señoritas* can—
we have a pillow fight
and jump on my queen-size bed.

"That's enough!"
Analiza yells from her room.
"¡Duérmanse!"

"No!" we shout together,
ignoring the fact that she wants
us to settle down
and rolling off the bed
in an avalanche
of jubilant laughter.
We're still screaming wildly
when suddenly we hear something.
The two of us freeze
in a sisterly hug
and listen.

The phone is ringing.

We open the bedroom door
and creep into the hall warily
because it's three o'clock
in the morning.

Except for Analiza and us,
everyone is asleep.
Only the kitchen light is on,
a wavering beacon
to which we are fearfully drawn.
Analiza stands there,
hands shaking
as she grips the phone,
pressing it against her ear,
then returns it to its cradle.
Her hair is disheveled,
like a tumbleweed.
Through her curls, her face
is stained with anguish.

Our bare feet cold
on the old linoleum,
we huddle and cry together,
fingers, hands, and arms
all intertwined.
We are tangled up
like three rambling rose vines
yet torn apart inside.

Analiza tries to speak,
but the words get caught
in a snare of sobs.
She doesn't have to say it.
We know.
Mami's gone.

mi madre

On Mami's grave
lies a tiny, tin nameplate,
inexpensive and unrefined,
an understated
grave marker for a woman
who meant so much
to six daughters,
two sons, and her
beloved husband.
Mi madre
was faceted
like a diamond.

Sometimes
she was a *sirena*,

an enchanting mermaid,
harmonizing
along with the radio
when she thought
she was alone.
Her melody called us
away from our friends.
We stood with
our faces pressed
against the window screen,
loving the sound of her voice
as she sang with passion,
like Selena,
una canción de amor.

Sometimes
she was as comfortable
as a blanket,
enveloping us
in her warmth.
She was so soft,
we never wanted
to let her go.

Other times
she was *peligrosa*
as a scorpion.
We had to be careful,
because she'd pinch us
to keep us quiet
in church.

One time
when I was ten years old,
she was *loca*, a wild rebel
in polyester shorts
riding my bicycle barefoot
up the street.
We were so embarrassed.

But this morning,
at the viewing,
mi madre was as silent
as a statue: cold
and perfectly still,
waxed in beauty
for eternity.

PART SIX

words on the wind

poems from under the mesquite

It's only been a month
since Mami's passing,
but even before that
it had been awhile since
she had been home and
well enough to tend her garden.
Without her touch,
no matter how much
we watered them,
one by one Mami's rosebushes
faded into the dirt.

Today is Día de las Madres.
If she were still with us,

we would be celebrating Mother's Day
by serenading Mami
with "*Las mañanitas*."
Instead, I am outside
looking for a sign from her.
Where her garden used to bloom,
dusty holes stare back at me
from the barren soil
of what is like a miniature graveyard.
But the mesquite
is as strong as ever.

I notice Papi
is watching me worriedly
from inside the house.
He keeps looking at me as if
I am a ripened fruit
dangling from a dead vine.
I think he's afraid
that I'm going to fall
when he's not there to catch me,
afraid I'm going to hit the ground
hard and keep rolling,
get lost in the brush—rot.

Only I know that won't happen.
No matter how bad things get,
I can always be found here,
planted firmly in what's left
of Mami's rose garden,
with a pen in my hand,
leaning against this same sturdy trunk,
still writing poems
in the shade of the mesquite.

changes

Summer after senior year

In our yard, clusters of
tasseled, yellow flowers
are beginning to blossom
on the mesquite.
Later they'll give way
to tender, slender pods.

Spring brought a few surprises.
Victoria and I placed at District
and at Regionals in Dramatic Duet,
then went on to the Area competition.
We didn't make the finals
at State despite everyone's
predictions that we would.

But we did go to my prom—
Analiza and Victoria had dates
who were seniors, and even I
decided to dress up for once
and go with a date,
so all of us went together.
Mami would have loved
our frilly dresses.

I graduated last month,
and the world around me
is blooming brightly.
I know there will be
many more milestones
to celebrate.

Inside, though, I am
still caught in a swamp,
trying to trudge my way
through the devastating loss
I feel with Mami gone.
Even with the support
of our friends and family,

waking up every day,
cooking, eating, sleeping,
even breathing is a struggle.

When I started back at school
after Mami's funeral,
I went to talk with Mr. Cortés.
He told me how sorry he was
and asked me how I was managing.
"Have you been able to
keep up with your courses?"

"School's going fine," I answered.
"Homework actually helps—
you know, having something else
to keep my mind busy.
It's my emotions I worry about.
I'm afraid I'm going to break down
if anyone asks me how I'm—feeling."

I pressed a finger into the inner corner
of my eye and took a long, deep breath.
We looked out the window together

and watched the rain come down
hard on the quad.
After a while Mr. Cortés
turned to me and said,
"Lupita, no matter how much it rains,
the roads won't stay flooded.
Eventually everything dries out again.
It just takes awhile."

Now summer is here, and Papi
is working again, as busy as
a carpenter ant, working with his crew
building a mall at the end of our street.
Mireya and Sarita are going
away to college in the fall.
I can't even begin
to make plans like that right now.
No. I live in a bog so dense
it dampens my every thought.

In a way I'm glad
it's all over—the responsibility,
the stress, the hospital stays.

I feel guilty, yet part of me
is secretly relieved
that some of the heaviness
has been lifted off us.
My sisters are free now,
free to be social butterflies,
free to wear soft, satin dresses
and high-heeled shoes
at *bailes* and *Quinceañeras*,
free to dance the night away.

But as for me,
how can I move on
when I'm so confused
by my own emotions?
How am I supposed to enjoy life
when Mami isn't here
to share it with us?
One moment I'm thankful
she's finally at rest,
and the next I'm missing her
so much, I sit around pretending
she's still here

watching and listening,
only unable to speak to us.
Then reality hits me, and I feel
as if I must be losing my mind,
imagining things like that.

Even writing doesn't help me
sort through things anymore.

Tonight when I'm outside
under the mesquite
watching stars bejewel the sky,
Papi comes over
and sits down next to me.

"I know how you feel," he volunteers,
even though I've never shared
my innermost thoughts with him.
"It's like you're stuck,
just sitting here under this tree,
thinking about your *mami*.
It's okay to ponder life, Lupita,
but you can't mourn forever.

Mami wouldn't want that.
You have to start living again."

Papi thinks I need a change
of scenery. He tells me
I can go visit his mother
in Mexico, *mi abuela* Hortencia.
He wants me to go back
and talk to my childhood friends,
be close to the people
and things I grew up with,
spend time in nature,
go out at night
just to watch the fireflies
create their own daylight in the dark
the way I used to
when I was young.

I tell him I'll go, although
I don't see how any of it
is going to make a difference.

at abuelita's house

Piedras Negras, Coahuila, Mexico

I cross the border
sitting beside Papi in silence.
The fiery wind burns my cheeks,
and my long hair whips
my face and neck.

But when Papi drops me off,
mi abuelita's house
is cool and breezy, welcoming.
I shake out the contents
of my bag onto a cot
set up in her laundry room.

In the mornings when I awaken
in that sky-blue room,

with its ancient walls
simply sloughing off the years,
I lie in bed and listen
to the music of a water leak
coming from the spigot on the wall.

At Abuelita's house
I find a new rhythm,
getting up at dawn to help
Tío Manuelito feed the chickens
and collect their brown eggs.
Afterward I sit on the porch steps
and look across the sparse
scrap of a backyard
at the tiny blue house
we used to call home.
It is old and ruinous,
like a shipwreck;
but playful children
keep swimming in and out of it,
laughing blissfully.

Here, in the town where I was born,
I drink in the late-summer

afternoons and the coolness
of the tangy *agua de tamarindo*
my childhood friend Ofelia
offers me, filling my glass
from a fat-bellied
glass barrel on the counter
of her parents' store.

When Ofelia and I talk
of the future, she asks,
"What are you going to do
with your life, Lupita?"
Like me, she's seventeen years old;
but she already runs
her parents' *comercio*, the store
which will become her own
when she gets married next spring.

"I don't know," I say. "I just know
I'm not ready to get married
and start having kids of my own.
There are so many more things
I want to do before I settle down
to raise a family."

"Like what?" she asks,
and I think seriously
about what I want.

"I used to imagine myself
moving to New York
to be in a Broadway show,
or becoming a photojournalist
and backpacking through Europe,"
I say, remembering it all.
"I had so many dreams
Mami and I used to talk about:
community college,
a career, traveling.
She wanted so much
to see me do those things.
But now that she's gone,
what's the point?"

Ofelia teasingly calls me
la aventurera sin moneda
because I've told her
I'll have to make my own money

as I go along now that
all our savings are gone.
She probably thinks I'm crazy
for even considering leaving home;
but she hugs me and tells me,
"Everything will be all right.
You'll figure it out."

I nod my head and smile,
because a part of me
is beginning to believe
that she's right. Someday I will
figure things out.

At Abuelita's house
time stands still,
holds its breath,
and leaves me alone
so I can think.

One afternoon I scrub
my bedsheets against
Abuelita's aluminum washboard,

then hang them up on the clothesline
and lie back lazily on the grass
while the sun dries them.
Suddenly the wind picks up.
I watch the sheets' futile struggle
to hold their own
against the force of nature.
They flap and pull,
twirling themselves
in and out of frenzied knots.

The sight of those bedsheets
battling nature itself
as the wind starts to tear them
off the clothesline
makes me bolt into action.
Fighting the willful breeze,
I tug at the twisted sheets,
trying to smooth them out
and pin them back up
even as they thrash around me,
slapping at my arms,
covering my face, smothering me.

Abuelita Hortencia
runs out of the house
and comes to my rescue.
She grabs the damp sheets
as if by the scruff of their necks,
folds them quickly
against her stomach,
and drops them one by one
into an old wicker basket at her feet.

"They got dirty," I say,
noticing the dark soil stains
along the edges of the white cloth.
"I'll wash them again."
I heave the wicker basket up
and anchor it against my hip bone
as if it were a toddler
attached to my side.

Abuelita nods and says,
"Sometimes it's best to take things down
and start all over again.
It's the way of the world, Lupita.

No use fighting it."
Then she gives me a kiss on the cheek
and walks away, going into the house
without looking back.

Standing there with nothing
but the mute wind
to keep me company,
at last I feel something unfurl within me.
Like a shoot growing
from what remains—a tiny piece
of buried mesquite root—
determination flourishes.

The air grows calmer,
sighing softly all around me
as I put down the basket.
I sit on the grass,
reach for my journal,
and start to tear out pages.
I rip out all the sad, tortured
poems I've written
since Mami's funeral

and pile them on the ground
in front of me. I'm wondering
what to do with them
when, without warning,
as if deciding for me,
the wild wind kicks up again
and scatters the tattered
pages everywhere.
Like freed carrier pigeons, they fly—
getting farther and farther away from me
until I can't see them anymore.

Laughter, like a cleansing rain,
pours out of me.
After everything that's happened,
and everything that hasn't,
it hurts, but it also feels good
finally to let Mami go.

Later I find a tall mesquite
to sit under;
and with my pen in hand,
I open my journal

to a blank page and begin
writing a whole new batch of poems,
poems filled with memories
and hope, because that's
what Mami would've wanted.

homecoming

"You ready to come home?"
It's the third time my father has come
to Abuela Hortencia's house
asking me the same question.

Today I finally nod my head
and gather my belongings.

"Your sisters are growing up,"
he tells me as we trundle home
in his prehistoric pickup.
"Analiza and Victoria are dating now."

I raise my eyebrows
as if I didn't know.

"Always the last one
to find out," I murmur.

Papi laughs, a sound
like a roiling river. Then he pats
my hand and pulls into the *aduana*
at the International Bridge.

"Did you enjoy your vacation?"
Papi asks, looking at me.

"Yes," I say, keeping my eyes
on the dashboard, not yet ready
to discuss my future. "Did you?"

He laughs again. This time
the river runs slow, almost playfully,
in the back of his throat.
"We managed," he concedes,
and then he pays the toll.

permission

It is as if Papi has suddenly
developed Alzheimer's.
My meticulous father has forgotten
where he put last year's tax records.
At least that's what he claims
every time I ask him to help me
fill out my financial aid form.

"What happened to staying home
and going to community college?"
Papi asks. "There's a reason girls
shouldn't go away to college.
Predators lurk on those campuses!"
Papi blusters, waving
a college catalog in his fist
like banned literature at a book burning.

"Oh yes," I tease him, "and let's not forget
    the Lechuza and the boogeyman!
    Papi—I'm not a child anymore!"

"Listen," he says, his green eyes
    as intense as polished agate stones.
"I made promises to your mother.
    I told her I'd take good care of you,
    put you all before myself or anyone else.
    Lupita, *m'ija*, there's no place
    safer than home."

"But I want to go places
    where I can see new things
    and meet new people," I argue.
"I want a chance to explore
    the rest of *los Estados Unidos*.
    I can't help it, Papi. I'm like you!
    You were a teenager
    when you first left Mexico
    and came to this country.
    And look at what you've built.
    This family. This home.

All the construction
projects you've worked on.
Now it's my turn to go out
and do something on my own."

I've been begging for weeks,
a relentless mosquito
buzzing in his ear. This morning
Papi has finally decided:
"Lupita, I can't let you go."

the bus ticket

"But how?" Papi asks,
  looking at me as if the bus ticket
  in my hand is a razor blade
  I'm holding up to his throat.

"I found the tax forms
  inside Mami's old purse,
  copied the information, and
  mailed off the paperwork.
  I'm all set to go."

I can see by the look in his eyes
  he hates that I'm not
  honoring his decision.
  Still, I'm glad I finally told him.

Going behind his back
bothered me because
I love him so much.
But for a long time now
I've been dormant,
like the cicadas that wait
seventeen years before they emerge
from the ground.

"Papi, I had to do it," I explain.
"I'm ready to start my life."

For the first time since Mami's funeral,
my father cries. He looks down
at his hands, shakes his head,
and grabs at his chest. I feel ashamed,
like Malinche when she walked
away from her own city, Tenochtitlán.

I try to tell him it will be okay,
but the words in my throat
have turned to sawdust.
There's no dulling his pain;

I might as well
go jump in the Rio Grande.
We stand there for another minute
before he turns to go.

"Cash in your ticket," he tells me
as he leaves the kitchen.
"Buy yourself a coat.
It gets cold up there."

in the parking lot

Alpine, Texas

Papi restarts the engine
and gets out just long enough
to hug me tight, caress my hair,
and say *hasta luego*,
because *adiós* would be too hard.
Then he climbs in and
drives away, wiping his face,
leaving me standing
alone in the parking lot
outside my college dorm.
I watch him getting smaller
and smaller. *Me puede mucho—*
my heart aches for him.
I feel bad adding the weight

of another good-bye,
as if one loss wasn't enough
for him to endure in one year.
Still, I wipe my tears
and force myself to turn around.

This is a welcomed uprooting
for me. I am transplanting myself
to a whole new place,
with a new kind of language to learn.
Windows, like bright eyes, peer at me
curiously. I must be a sight,
only one suitcase and no purse.
Enough money in my back pocket
to feed me today. Tomorrow
is another story.

In the crisp mountain air,
a handful of scattered papers
swirl and dance, and I'm reminded of
that afternoon at Abuelita's house
when I tore out my old poems.
Now, seeing the loose pages

blowing around the parking lot
like fallen leaves, I can't help
but smile. I know what it's like
to wish the wind would lift me up
and transport me.
Someday my words will
take flight and claim the sky.

I don't know where I'll go from here,
but I want to make my own way.
This feels right to me—
starting to walk toward the doors,
holding Mami's old, blue suitcase,
and remembering
the love I carry with me.

ACKNOWLEDGMENTS

First, I would like to thank my family, especially my husband, Jim, and our three sons for giving me the time and space I needed to work on my writing. James, Steven, and Jason—you are the three greatest sons a mother could ever have. It has truly been an honor to be your mother. Each and every day I thank the Lord for the gift of you.

Second, I want to acknowledge a great editor, Emily Hazel, who read my small collection of poems and believed in it. She diligently, patiently, and devotedly helped me shape it and mold it until it became a novel in verse. Thank you for believing in me, Emily. I owe you the world.

Thanks also to my friends and colleagues at Christa McAuliffe Middle School, who have supported me and encouraged me throughout this entire process. Special thanks to my best friend, Sharon Boyd, a fellow poet, for reading every one of these poems and sharing her grammatical wisdom with me. A great, big thank-you to Sara Castro and Yolanda Escalera for so graciously reviewing and lending their language expertise in the revision of terms included at the back of the book.

Finally, my heartfelt appreciation and gratitude to the teachers at Eagle Pass ISD who helped me become the person I am today. Special thanks to Mr. Eddie Cruz, Ms. Evelyn Urbina, Ms. Lilia Moses, Ms. Diana Moses, Ms. Bertha Garcia, Ms. Esther Barrientos, and many, many more who shaped my life with love, courage, and wisdom. Bless you for genuinely caring about me and my family—my sisters and brothers, my father and mother—and for always making sure that I wasn't just learning but had everything I needed to succeed. You are my heroes because you gave so much and expected nothing in return: *mil gracias*, from the bottom *de mi corazón*.

NAMES, SPANISH WORDS,
AND CULTURAL REFERENCES

The following entries include pronunciations of Spanish terms
that have been adapted for spoken American English. There
are many regional and cultural differences in word choice and
pronunciation among Spanish speakers in the United States.
Usages and pronunciations in this book approximate the way
Spanish is spoken by Mexican Americans today in the areas
where the story is set.

abuela (ah-BWEH-lah): grandmother

Abuela Hortencia (ah-BWEH-lah or-TEHN-see-ah): Lupita's
paternal grandmother

Abuela Inez (ah-BWEH-lah ee-NEHS): Lupita's maternal
grandmother

abuelita (ah-bweh-LEE-tah): affectionate form of *abuela*,
similar to "grandma"

adiós (ah-dee-OHS): good-bye

¿Adónde vas? (ah-DOHN-deh vahs): Where are you going?

aduana (ah-DWAH-nah): customs station at the United States entrance of a Mexican border town

agua de tamarindo (AH-gwah de tah-mah-REEN-doh): cold drink made from the tamarind plant

Alcatraz (AL-kuh-traz): Alcatraz Penitentiary, former maximum-security federal prison that was located on Alcatraz Island, off the coast of California

Alpine (AL-pahyn): college town in West Texas, about a five-hour drive northwest from Eagle Pass

amigo (ah-MEE-goh): male friend

amiguita (ah-mee-GEE-tah): close female friend, girlfriend

Analiza (ah-nah-LEE-sah): Lupita's sister, second born

amor (ah-MOR): love

Andromache (ann-DRAH-mah-key): in Greek mythology, wife of Hector, crown prince of Troy, and mother of Astyanax

antojada (ahn-toh-HAH-dah): experiencing food cravings due to pregnancy

Astyanax (ASS-tye-uh-nicks): in Greek mythology, son of Hector, crown prince of Troy, and Andromache; during the Trojan War, the city of Troy was attacked, Hector was killed, and the child Astyanax was thrown from the city walls

Avenida López Mateos (ah-veh-NEE-dah LOH-pehs mah-TEH-ohs): López Mateos Avenue, a street in the city of Piedras Negras, Coahuila, Mexico

¡Ay, chihuahua! (aye chee-WAH-wah): expression similar to "Darn it!"

¡Ay, sí! (aye see): expression similar to "Yeah, right!"

Aztec (AZ-tek): member of a Nahuatl-speaking people that founded the Mexican empire conquered by Cortés in 1521

baile (BAH-ee-leh): dance

bebé (beh-BEH): baby

Benito (beh-NEE-toh): Lupita's brother, youngest of eight siblings

burrito (boo-RREE-toh): flour tortilla filled with meat, beans, and/or cheese

calcetín (kal-seh-TEEN): sock

canción de amor (kahn-see-OHN deh ah-MOR): love song

cariño (kah-REE-nyoh): tenderness, the special kind of love parents have for their children

carretera (kah-rreh-TEH-rah): highway

cascabel (kahs-kah-BEL): rattlesnake

catechism (KAT-i-kiz-uhm): instruction in the basic principles of Roman Catholic doctrine

chicharra (chee-CHA-rrah): cicada; large, winged insect common in many parts of the United States; the male produces a loud, buzzing sound; the seventeen-year periodical cicada burrows into the earth after hatching and develops underground, resurfacing after seventeen years to shed its hard outer skeleton and emerge as an adult

chimenea (chee-meh-NEH-ah): fireplace or hearth

chisme (CHEEZ-meh): gossip

chismosa (cheez-MOH-sah): person fond of gossiping

Christmas parade (KRIS-muhs puh-REYD): in celebration of Día de Nuestra Señora de Guadalupe, Our Lady of Guadalupe Day, on December 12 and the following days leading up to Christmas Day, folk dancers costumed as Aztecs perform traditional religious dances in a parade

cicada (si-KAY-duh *or* si-KAH-duh): see *chicharra*

cinco hermanitas (SEEN-koh ehr-mah-NEE-tahs): five little sisters

Coahuila (coh-ah-WEE-lah): northern Mexican state (formally Coahuila de Zaragoza) that borders Texas

cochinilla (coh-chee-NEE-yah): roly-poly, or pill bug

comadre (coh-MAH-dreh): close female friend, sometimes also godmother

comercio (coh-MEHR-see-oh): general store

como ardilla listada (COH-moh ar-DEE-yah lees-TAH-dah): like a chipmunk

como bandidas (COH-moh bahn-DEE-dahs): like bandits

compadre (com-PAH-dreh): close male friend, sometimes also godfather

confirmation (con-fer-MEY-shuhn): Christian rite of passage in which young people, usually around the age of fifteen, confirm their faith and are anointed as a sign of inward spiritual transformation, thus becoming full-fledged members of a church congregation

coqueta (coh-KEH-tah): coquettish, flirtatious

corazón (coh-rah-SOHN): heart

Cortés (kor-TEZ): last name of Lupita's drama teacher

de (deh): of

Día de las Madres (DEE-ah deh lahs MAH-drehs):
Mother's Day

Día de Nuestra Señora de Guadalupe (DEE-ah deh
NWEHS-trah seh-NYOH-rah deh gwah-dah-LOO-peh):
Our Lady of Guadalupe Day, a major holiday celebrated
on December 12, honoring Mexico's patron saint, the
Virgin of Guadalupe, who is believed to have miraculously
appeared to a Mexican peasant named Juan Diego in 1531

Diosito (dee-oh-SEE-toh): our beloved God

Doña Pepita (DOH-nyah peh-PEE-tah): neighbor of
Lupita's family; *Doña* is a title of respect given to women
and may be used with either the first or full name

dos lloronas (dos yo-ROH-nahs): two weeping women

¡Duérmanse! (DWEHR-mahn-seh): Go to sleep!

Eagle Pass (EE-guhl pas): small town in southwestern Texas
that borders the city of Piedras Negras in Coahuila,
Mexico; also called El Águila

El Águila (el AH-gee-lah): nickname for Eagle Pass

elote (eh-LOH-teh): ear of sweet corn, corn on the cob

elotes calientitos (eh-LOH-tehs kah-lee-ehn-TEE-tohs):
piping hot ears of roasted corn

en (en): in

enchilada (en-chee-LAH-dah): rolled tortilla filled with
cheese and sometimes beef or chicken and baked covered
in red chili sauce

español (ehs-pah-NYOHL): Spanish

familia (fah-MEE-lee-ah): family

Gabriela (gah-bree-EH-lah): Lupita's cousin, daughter of paternal uncle Rodrigo

Galveston (GAL-vuh-stuhn): town located on Galveston Island, just off the Gulf Coast of Texas, about a six-and-a-half-hour drive east from Eagle Pass

girasol (hee-rah-SOL): sunflower

güero (GWEH-roh): blond or fair skinned

hasta luego (AHS-tah loo-EH-goh): until we meet again

Hecuba (HEK-yoo-bah): in Greek mythology, wife of King Priam of Troy and mother of many children, including Hector

hermosa (ehr-MOH-sah): beautiful

Houston (HYOO-stuhn): city in southeastern Texas, about a one-hour drive northwest from Galveston

huisache (wee-SAH-cheh): short, thorny tree with fernlike fronds, similar to a mesquite

Huitzilopochtli (weet-see-lo-POCHT-lee) *[Nahuatl]*: Aztec war god (later the sun god) to whom human prisoners were sacrificed daily

iglesia (ee-GLEH-see-ah): church

International Bridge (in-ter-NASH-uh-nul brij): Eagle Pass–Piedras Negras International Bridge, which crosses the Rio Grande, connecting the United States–Mexico border cities of Eagle Pass, Texas, and Piedras Negras, Coahuila

Jesucristo (heh-soo-CREES-toh): Jesus Christ

Juanita (hwah-NEE-tah): Lupita's sister, sixth born

Judas (JOO-duhs): Judas Iscariot, one of the twelve disciples, who is known for betraying Jesus

la aventurera sin moneda (lah ah-vehn-too-REH-rah seen moh-NEH-dah): the adventurer without money

la Feria (lah FEH-ree-ah): la Feria del Sol (the Festival of the Sun), commonly known as the Fair; a major annual celebration in Piedras Negras with industrial, commercial, agricultural, and cattle exhibitions, similar to a county fair

la Llorona (lah yoh-ROH-nah): The Weeping Woman, a character in Mexican folklore whose eternal penance for having drowned her children is to try to find them and who is said to carry off children who misbehave

la Muerte (lah MWEHR-teh): Death (feminine personification)

La víbora de la mar (lah VEE-boh-rah deh lah mahr): The Sea Serpent, a popular children's sing-along game in which children hold hands to form a chain that moves like a serpent as they weave their way around obstacles

las/los (lahs/los): the (plural)

"Las mañanitas" (las mah-nyah-NEE-tahs): traditional birthday song in Mexico, also sung to mothers, grandmothers, and godmothers on Mother's Day

Lechuza (leh-CHOO-sah): Barn Owl, also known as Ghost Owl; mythological creature in Mexican folklore that is said to have the body of a bird and the face of a witch and that is believed to punish evildoers

limonada (lee-moh-NAH-dah): lemonade

loca (LO-kah): crazy (feminine)

los Estados Unidos (los ehs-TAH-dohs oo-NEE-dohs): the United States (of America)

"Los tres cochinitos" (los trehs coh-chee-NEE-tohs): lullaby loosely based on the story "The Three Little Pigs"

lotería (loh-teh-REE-ah): popular board game in Mexico played with individual game boards called *tablas* and calling cards with images such as "la Sirena," The Mermaid

Lucía (loo-SEE-ah): one of Mami's close female friends

Lupita (loo-PEE-tah): narrator, eldest of eight siblings; short for Guadalupe

madre (MAH-dreh): mother

Malinche (mah-LEEN-cheh): Aztec princess who betrayed her people and handed over the Aztec kingdom to the Spanish conquistador Hernán Cortés

mamá (muh-MAH): mother

mami (MAH-mee): affectionate form of *mamá*, similar to "mommy"

manita (mah-NEE-tah): term of endearment meaning "beloved sister"

matachines (mah-tah-CHEE-nehs): group of folk dancers colorfully costumed as Aztecs who perform in heavily Mexican American-populated areas of the southwestern United States during major Roman Catholic holidays; their dance reflects aspects of Spanish, Mexican, and Native American cultures combined with Roman Catholic tradition, and the theme is the eternal battle between good and evil

Me puede mucho. (meh PWEH-deh MOO-choh): I feel
  it deeply.

melancolía (meh-lahn-coh-LEE-ah): sadness, melancholy

mercado (mehr-KAH-doh): marketplace

merienda (meh-ree-EHN-dah): a light snack in the afternoon;
  teatime

mesquite (meh-SKEET *or* MES-keet): tree with beanlike
  pods, sharp thorns, and extraordinarily long roots native
  to the southwestern United States and northern Mexico,
  known for its ability to survive in harsh climates

mesquite meal (meh-SKEET meel *or* MES-keet meel):
  naturally sweet, high-protein flour made by grinding
  dried mesquite pods and seeds; also used as a spice

mi (mee): my

m'ija (MEE-hah): term of endearment meaning
  "beloved daughter"

mil gracias (meel GRAH-see-ahs): many thanks

Mireya (mee-REH-yah): Lupita's best friend, twin sister
  of Sarita

mole (MOH-leh): rich, brown sauce made of chili peppers,
  spices, chocolate, and peanut butter, usually served with
  chicken or turkey

mosquitas muertas (mohs-KEE-tahs MWER-tahs): dead
  flies; slang term referring to deceptive, scheming females

muchachita (moo-chah-CHEE-tah): little girl

mujeres (moo-HEH-rehs): women

muñeca (moo-NYEH-kah): doll

muy rico y picoso (MOO-ee RREE-co ee pee-COH-soh): very good and spicy

Nahuatl (NAH-waht-l): language spoken by the Aztecs (also known as the Nahua), an ancient people native to central Mexico

nene (NEH-neh): baby boy

niña (NEE-nyah): little girl

nopalera (no-pah-LEH-rah): cluster or field of cacti

nopales en salsa (no-PAH-lehs ehn SAHL-sah): stewlike dish made with cacti, skinned and sautéed in a spicy, tomato-based sauce

Nuestra Señora de Guadalupe (NWEHS-trah seh-NYOH-rah deh gwah-dah-LOO-peh): El Santuario de Nuestra Señora de Guadalupe, or The Sanctuary of Our Lady of Guadalupe, a Catholic church in Piedras Negras, Coahuila, Mexico

Ofelia (oh-FEH-lee-ah): Lupita's childhood girlfriend who lives in Piedras Negras, Mexico

ojito (oh-HEE-toh): slang term for "creek" or "stream"

Paco (PAH-coh): Lupita's brother, fourth born

papi (PAH-pee): affectionate form of *papá*, similar to "daddy"

Pedro Infante (PEH-droh in-FAHN-teh): Mexican actor and singer (1917–1957), one of the most famous performers during the Golden Age of Mexican Cinema (1935–1959)

peligrosa (peh-lee-GROH-sah): dangerous

Piedras Negras (pee-EH-drahs NEH-grahs): city in the state of Coahuila, Mexico, located just across the border from Eagle Pass, Texas

pinole (pee-NOH-leh): treat made with toasted mesquite meal, sugar, and spices

plaza de toros (PLAH-sah deh TOH-rohs): bullfighting arena

Posadas (poh-SAH-dahs): *las Posadas*, a nine-day celebration with candlelit processions beginning on December 16 reenacting the part of the Christmas story in which Mary and Joseph search for lodging in Bethlehem

¡Qué talento! (keh tah-LEHN-toh): What talent!

Quinceañera (keen-seh-ah-NYEH-rah): celebration of a girl's fifteenth birthday, usually a large party, that is her formal social debut; a *quinceañera* is also a fifteen-year-old girl

ratoncita (rah-ton-SEE-tah): little female mouse; slang term for "petty thief"

rebozo (reh-BOH-soh): shawl, usually made of cotton, worn wrapped around the head and draped over the shoulders

rinconcito (reen-con-SEE-toh): tiny place, small niche

Rio Grande (REE-yoh GRAHN-deh): river that forms the border between northern Mexico and Texas; known in Mexico as the Río Bravo del Norte, or simply Río Bravo

Rosita (roh-SEE-tah): Lupita's sister, seventh born

Sacred Heart Church annex (SEY-krid hahrt church AN-iks): secondary building attached to the main building of the Sacred Heart Roman Catholic Church in Eagle Pass, Texas

salud (sah-LOOD): health

San Vicente (sahn vee-SEHN-teh): small town in the state of Coahuila, Mexico, located along the Rio Grande, about a one-hour drive south from Eagle Pass

Sarita (sah-REE-tah): twin sister of Lupita's best friend, Mireya

secreto (seh-CREH-toh): secret

Selena (seh-LEE-nah): Selena Quintanilla-Pérez, Texas-born Mexican American singer-songwriter known as the Queen of Tejano [Texan] Music

señorita (seh-nyoh-REE-tah): young lady; also a title given to an unmarried woman of any age

Serafina (seh-rah-FEE-nah): one of Mami's close female friends

serpiente (sehr-pee-EHN-teh): snake

sí (see): yes

sirena (see-REH-nah): mermaid

Spanish rice (SPAN-ish rahys): side dish prepared by sautéing dry rice, then cooking it in a tomato-based sauce made with chicken broth and spices; also known as Mexican rice

tabla (TAH-blah): individual game board, similar to a bingo card, used to play *lotería*

taco (TAH-koh): often crisply fried tortilla folded over a variety of fillings such as seasoned meat, lettuce, tomatoes, and cheese

Te quiero mucho. (teh kee-EH-roh MOO-choh): I love you very much.

telenovela (teh-leh-noh-VEH-lah): Mexican soap opera; also a general term for a Spanish-language soap opera featuring Latin American characters

Tenochtitlán (teh-nosh-teet-LAHN) *[Nahuatl]*: capital of the Aztec civilization; modern-day Mexico City, the capital of Mexico

tesoro (teh-SOH-roh): treasure

testal (tehs-TAHL): ball of dough to be made into a flour tortilla

"The Highwayman" (thuh HAHY-wey-muhn): famous narrative poem by Alfred Noyes about a highway robber who is in love with the landlord's daughter and is betrayed by a jealous rival

The Trojan Women (thuh TROH-juhn WIM-in): Greek tragedy written by Euripedes in 415 BCE; the third installment in a trilogy dealing with events and repercussions of the fall of Troy during and after the Trojan War

tía (TEE-ah): aunt

Tía Belén (TEE-ah beh-LEHN): one of Lupita's maternal aunts

Tía Maritza (TEE-ah mah-REET-zah): one of Lupita's maternal aunts

tío (TEE-oh): uncle

Tío Manuelito (TEE-oh mah-noo-eh-LEE-toh): one of Lupita's paternal uncles

Tío Rodrigo (TEE-oh roh-DREE-goh): one of Lupita's paternal uncles

Tío Saúl (TEE-oh sah-OOL): one of Lupita's paternal uncles

Tita (TEE-tah): Lupita's sister, fifth born

tortilla (tor-TEE-yah): thin, round bread made with flour or cornmeal, rolled flat, and usually served hot with a filling or topping

Trojan women (TROH-juhn WIM-in): characters in Greek mythology who lived in the city of Troy

Troy (troi): former city, in factual history and in legend, that was located in modern-day Turkey

UIL (yoo ahy el): University Interscholastic League, a Texas state competition league in which students compete in a wide range of team and individual events in academics, performing arts, and athletics; top contestants advance from the District level to Regionals, then to Area, and finally to State

una/un (OO-nah/oon): a

vago (VAH-go): vagabond or wanderer, lazy person

vaquero (vah-KEH-roh): cowboy

Venus flytrap (VEE-nuhs FLAHY-trap): carnivorous plant that has traps on the tips of its leaves for catching insects

Victoria (vik-TOH-ree-uh): Lupita's sister, third born

Virgen de Guadalupe (VEER-hen deh gwah-dah-LOO-peh): Virgin of Guadalupe, Mexico's patron saint, a Mexican Catholic image of the Virgin Mary